BLUESMAN

BOOK ONE

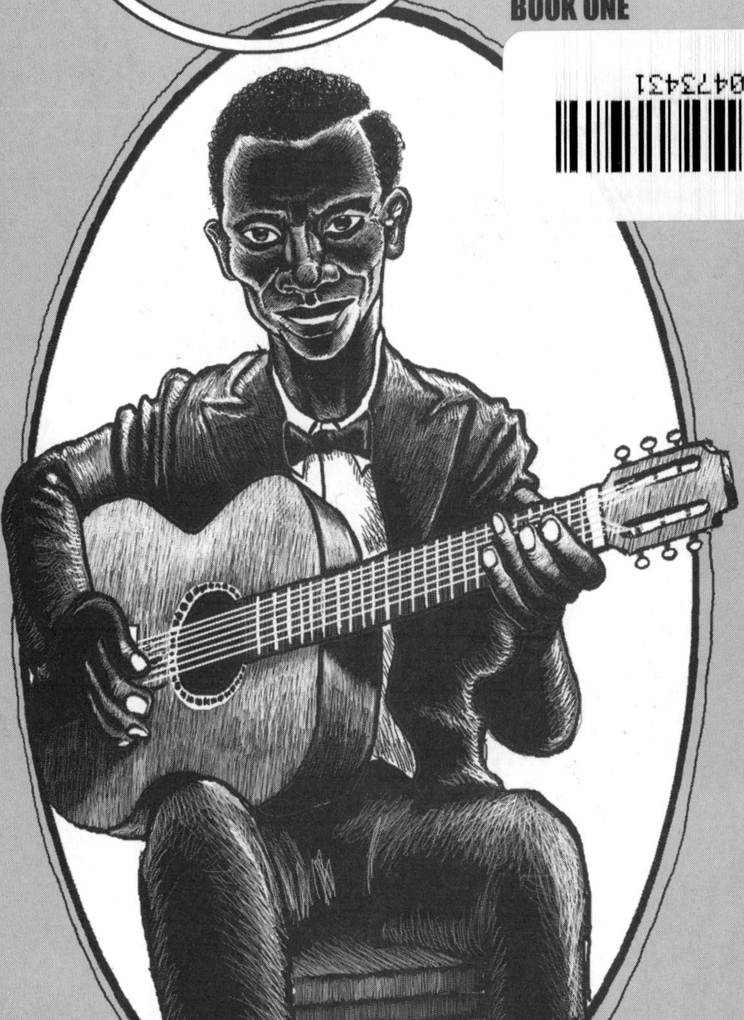

A twelve bar graphic narrative in the key of life and death.

BY ROB VOLLMAR & PABLO C. CALLEJO

Don't miss:
Bluesman, vol. 2, $8.95
Bluesman, vol. 3, $8.95 (July)

We have over 200
graphic novels in print,
write for our color catalog:
NBM
40 Exchange Place Suite 1308
New York, NY 10005
www.nbmpublishing.com

BLUESMAN
BOOK TWO
ROB VOLLMAR & PABLO G. CALLEJO

BLUESMAN
BOOK THREE
ROB VOLLMAR & PABLO G. CALLEJO

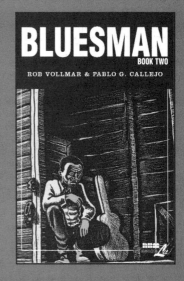

ISBN-10: 0-9742468-3-2
ISBN-13: 978-0-9742468-3-3

Printed in Canada

ComicsLit is an imprint
and trademark of

NANTIER • BEALL • MINOUSTCHINE
Publishing inc.
new york

1

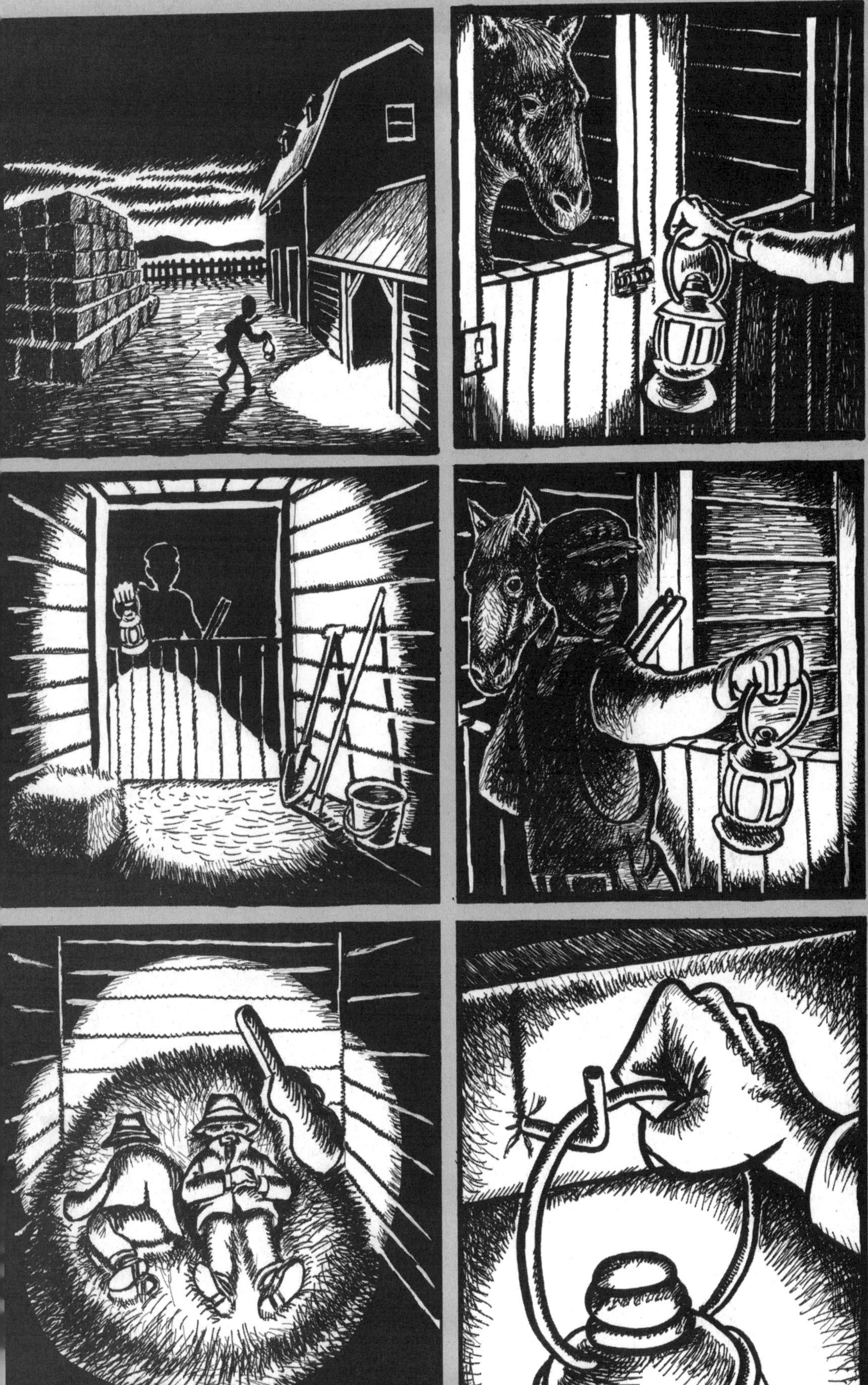

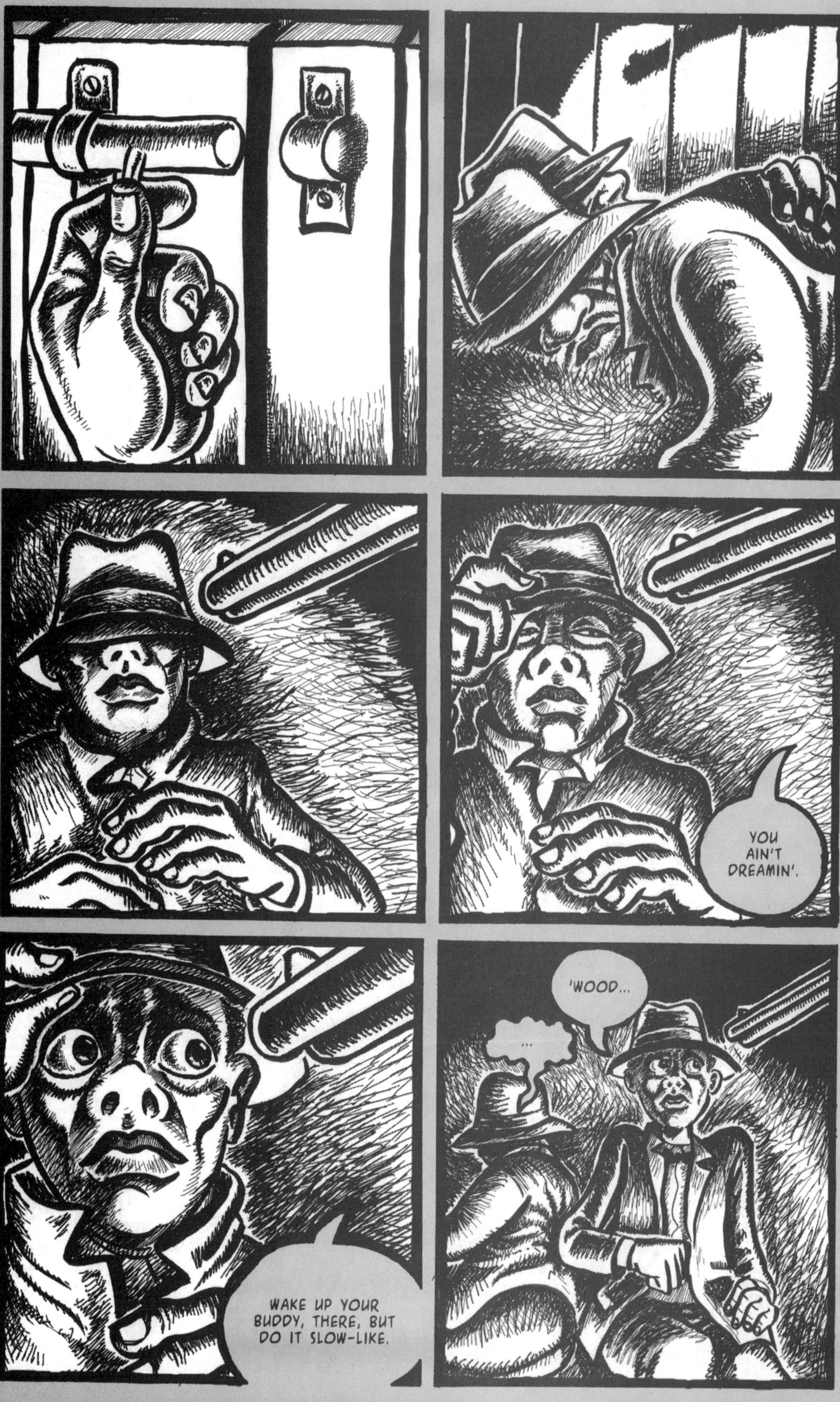
YOU AIN'T DREAMIN'.
WAKE UP YOUR BUDDY, THERE, BUT DO IT SLOW-LIKE.
'WOOD...
...

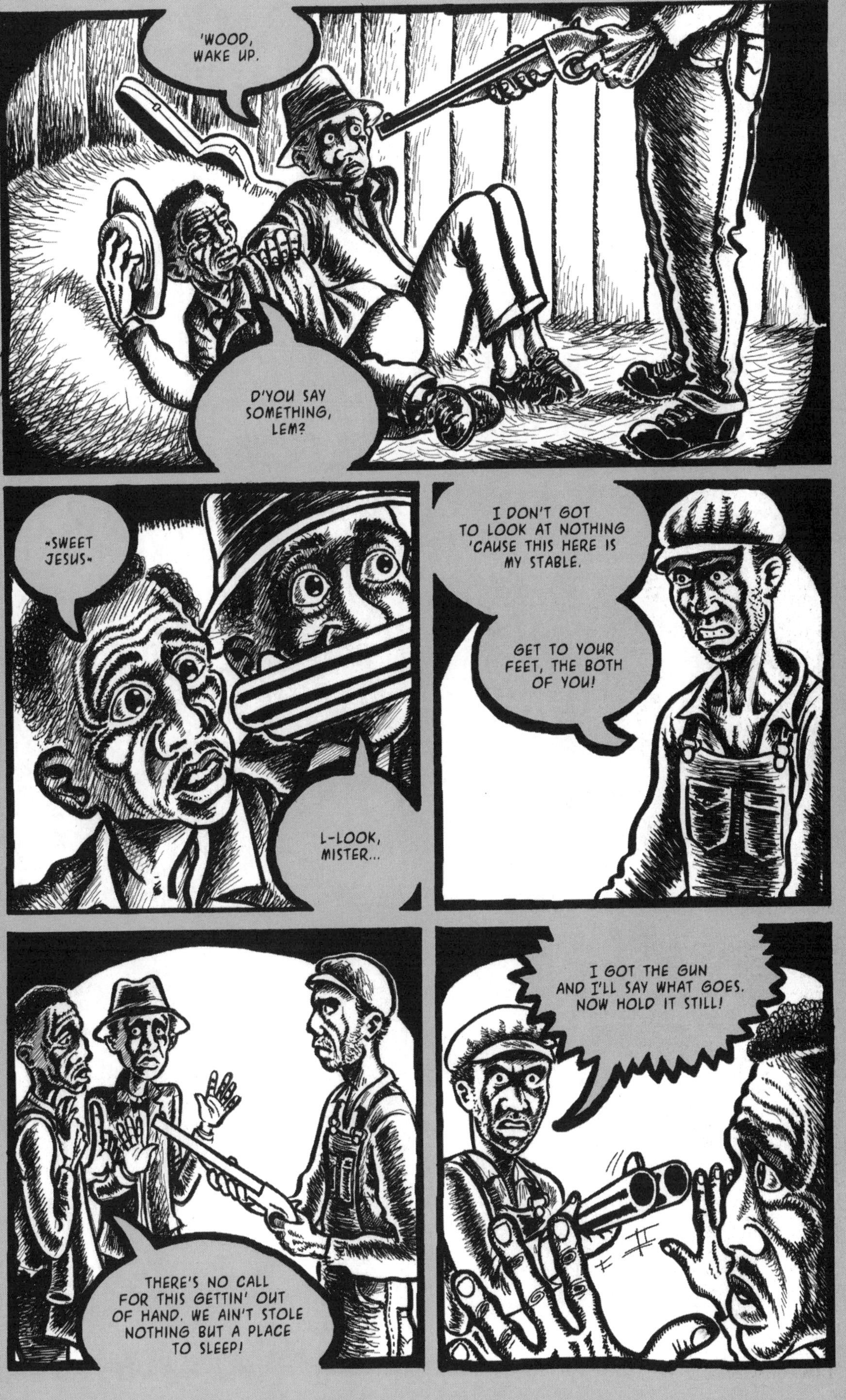
'WOOD, WAKE UP.
D'YOU SAY SOMETHING, LEM?
«SWEET JESUS»
L-LOOK, MISTER...
I DON'T GOT TO LOOK AT NOTHING 'CAUSE THIS HERE IS MY STABLE.
GET TO YOUR FEET, THE BOTH OF YOU!
THERE'S NO CALL FOR THIS GETTIN' OUT OF HAND. WE AIN'T STOLE NOTHING BUT A PLACE TO SLEEP!
I GOT THE GUN AND I'LL SAY WHAT GOES. NOW HOLD IT STILL!

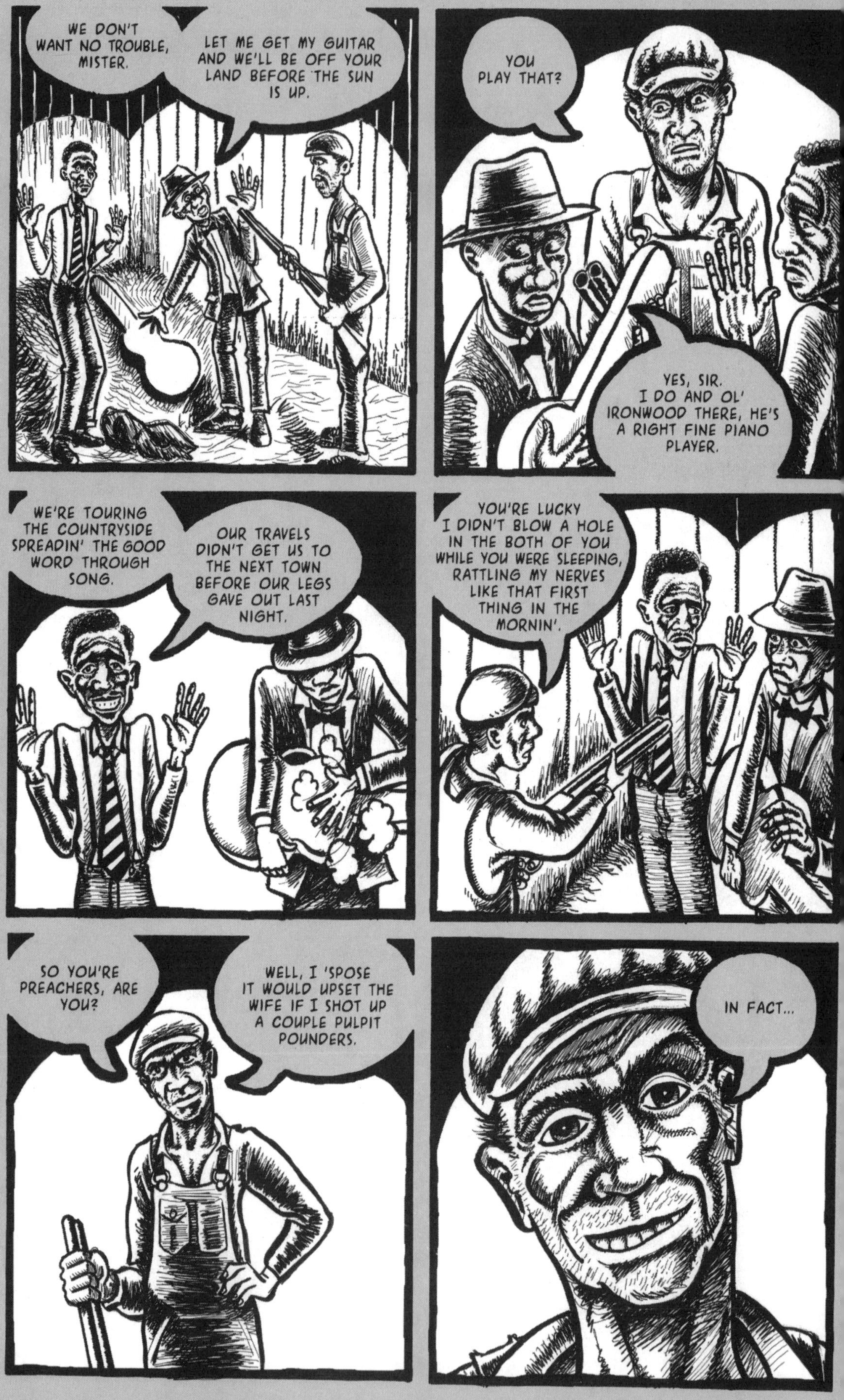
WE DON'T WANT NO TROUBLE, MISTER.
LET ME GET MY GUITAR AND WE'LL BE OFF YOUR LAND BEFORE THE SUN IS UP.
YOU PLAY THAT?
YES, SIR. I DO AND OL' IRONWOOD THERE, HE'S A RIGHT FINE PIANO PLAYER.
WE'RE TOURING THE COUNTRYSIDE SPREADIN' THE GOOD WORD THROUGH SONG.
OUR TRAVELS DIDN'T GET US TO THE NEXT TOWN BEFORE OUR LEGS GAVE OUT LAST NIGHT.
YOU'RE LUCKY I DIDN'T BLOW A HOLE IN THE BOTH OF YOU WHILE YOU WERE SLEEPING, RATTLING MY NERVES LIKE THAT FIRST THING IN THE MORNIN'.
SO YOU'RE PREACHERS, ARE YOU?
WELL, I 'SPOSE IT WOULD UPSET THE WIFE IF I SHOT UP A COUPLE PULPIT POUNDERS.
IN FACT...

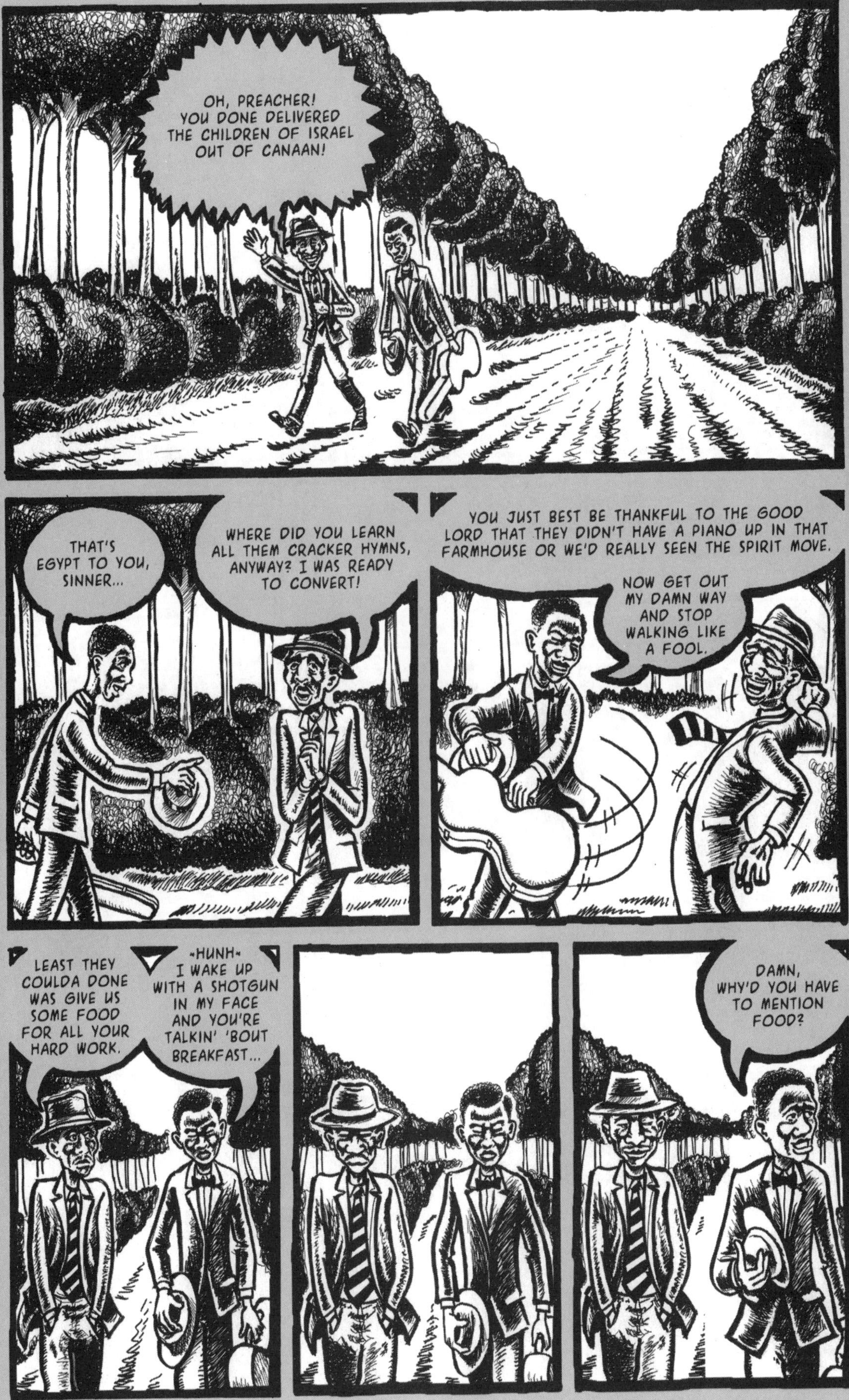
OH, PREACHER! YOU DONE DELIVERED THE CHILDREN OF ISRAEL OUT OF CANAAN!
THAT'S EGYPT TO YOU, SINNER...
WHERE DID YOU LEARN ALL THEM CRACKER HYMNS, ANYWAY? I WAS READY TO CONVERT!
YOU JUST BEST BE THANKFUL TO THE GOOD LORD THAT THEY DIDN'T HAVE A PIANO UP IN THAT FARMHOUSE OR WE'D REALLY SEEN THE SPIRIT MOVE.
NOW GET OUT MY DAMN WAY AND STOP WALKING LIKE A FOOL.
LEAST THEY COULDA DONE WAS GIVE US SOME FOOD FOR ALL YOUR HARD WORK.
«HUNH» I WAKE UP WITH A SHOTGUN IN MY FACE AND YOU'RE TALKIN' 'BOUT BREAKFAST...
DAMN, WHY'D YOU HAVE TO MENTION FOOD?

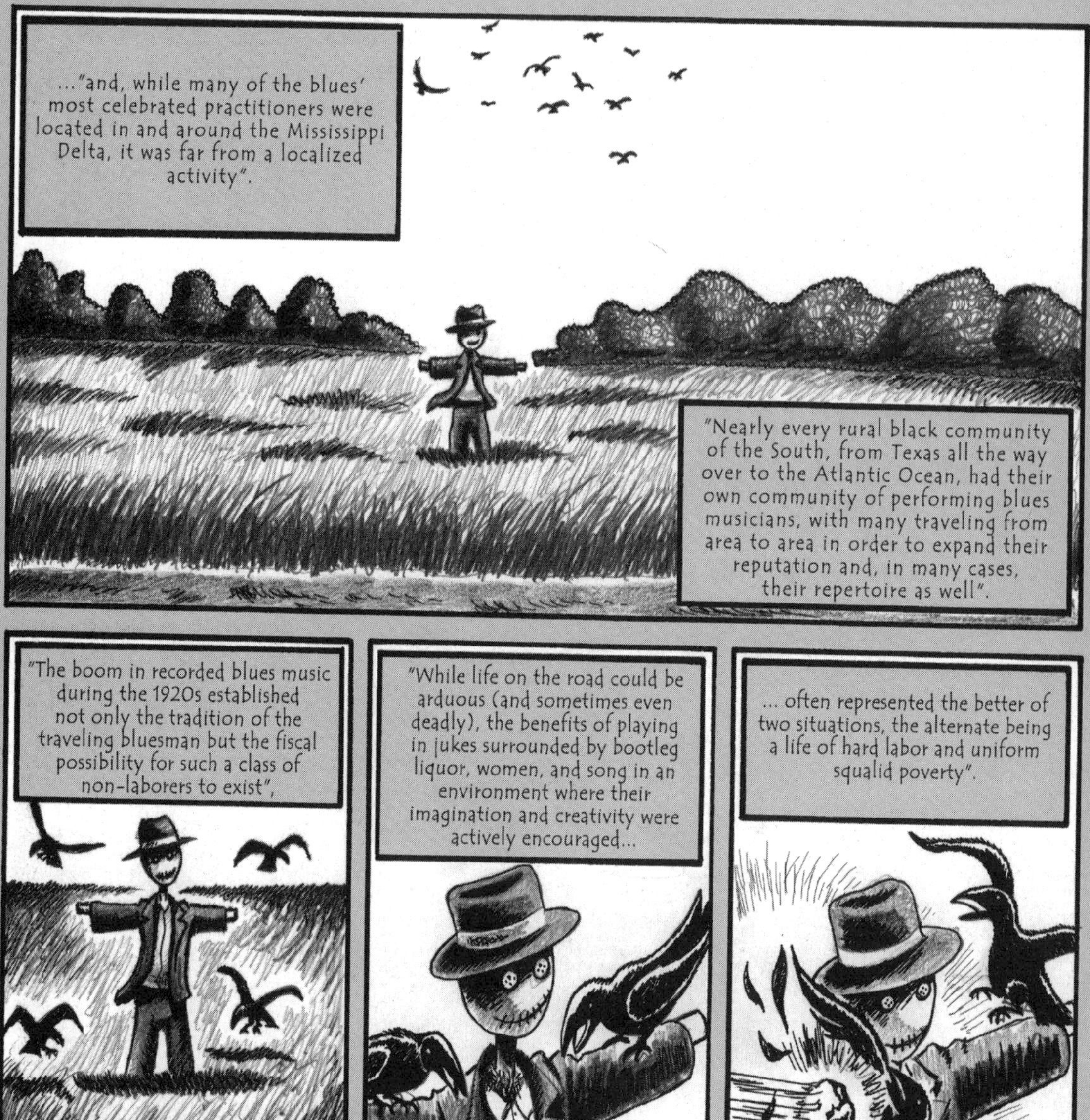
..."and, while many of the blues' most celebrated practitioners were located in and around the Mississippi Delta, it was far from a localized activity".
"Nearly every rural black community of the South, from Texas all the way over to the Atlantic Ocean, had their own community of performing blues musicians, with many traveling from area to area in order to expand their reputation and, in many cases, their repertoire as well".
"The boom in recorded blues music during the 1920s established not only the tradition of the traveling bluesman but the fiscal possibility for such a class of non-laborers to exist",
"While life on the road could be arduous (and sometimes even deadly), the benefits of playing in jukes surrounded by bootleg liquor, women, and song in an environment where their imagination and creativity were actively encouraged...
... often represented the better of two situations, the alternate being a life of hard labor and uniform squalid poverty".
"This privileged status, pocked as it was by chronically poor living conditions for these itinerant musicians, over time fostered a love-hate relationship with the communities they serviced".
"To the rural black society of this diverse region of the South, these bluesmen represented both an escape from their misery and an easy target on whom to pin the negative attributes uniformly assigned to all members of their race by the Anglo dominated society which surrounded them".

[Excerpted from Ira Deldoff's "America's Troubadors: Blues Musicians of the Deep South 1900-present", Real Folk Quarterly, March 1961]

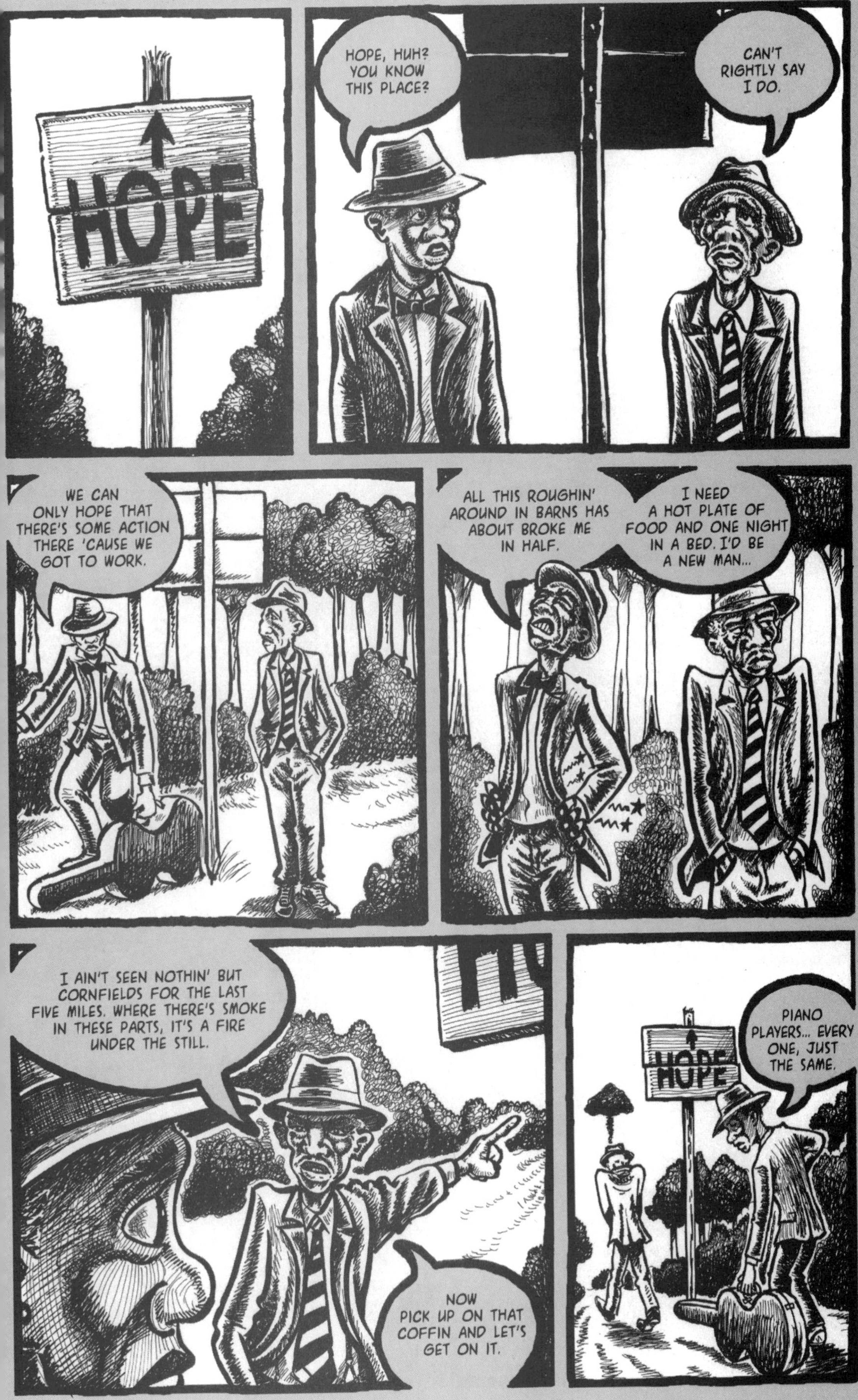
HOPE
HOPE, HUH? YOU KNOW THIS PLACE?
CAN'T RIGHTLY SAY I DO.
WE CAN ONLY HOPE THAT THERE'S SOME ACTION THERE 'CAUSE WE GOT TO WORK.
ALL THIS ROUGHIN' AROUND IN BARNS HAS ABOUT BROKE ME IN HALF.
I NEED A HOT PLATE OF FOOD AND ONE NIGHT IN A BED. I'D BE A NEW MAN...
I AIN'T SEEN NOTHIN' BUT CORNFIELDS FOR THE LAST FIVE MILES. WHERE THERE'S SMOKE IN THESE PARTS, IT'S A FIRE UNDER THE STILL.
NOW PICK UP ON THAT COFFIN AND LET'S GET ON IT.
HOPE
PIANO PLAYERS... EVERY ONE, JUST THE SAME.

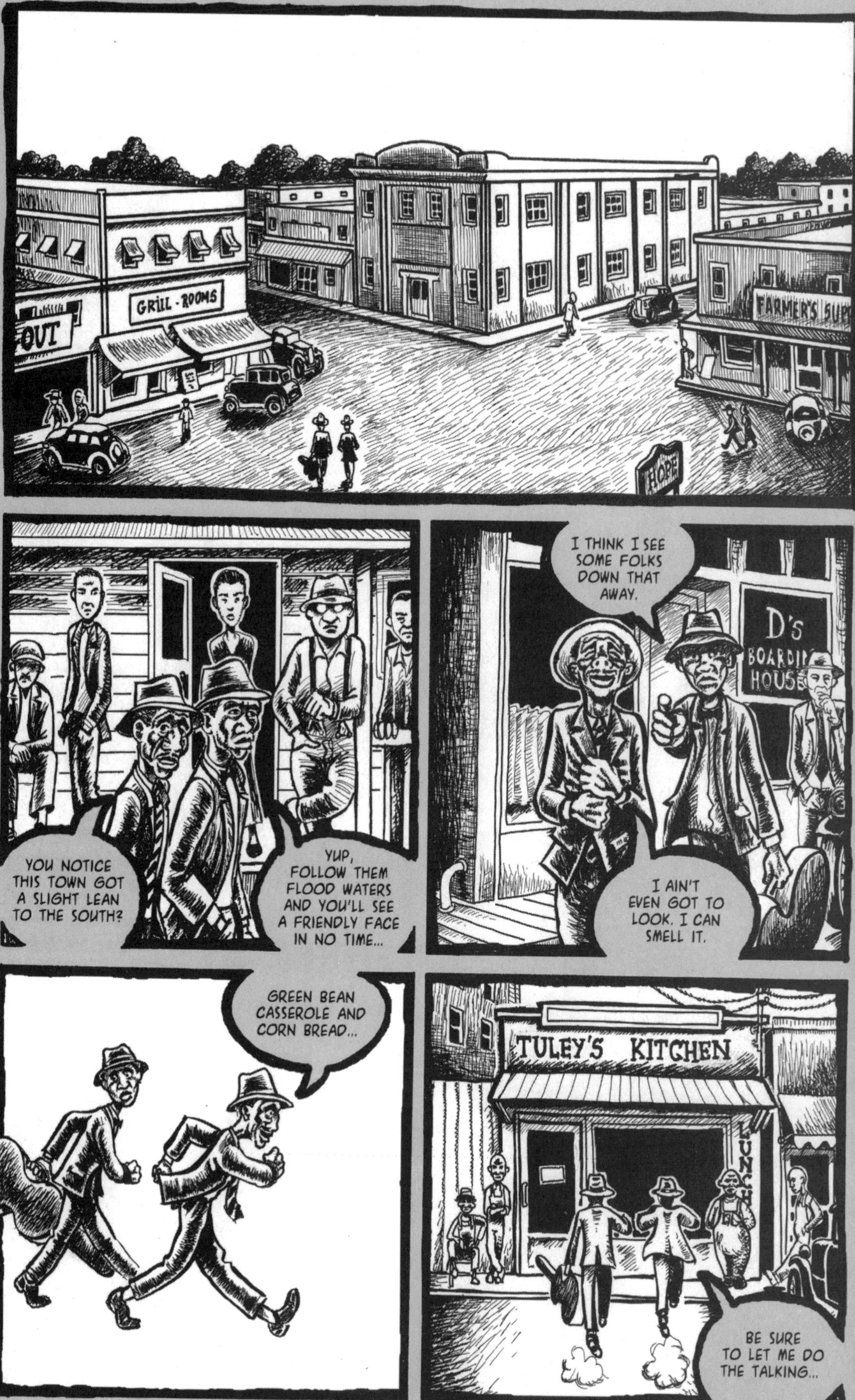
GRILL - ROOMS
OUT
FARMER'S SUP
HOPE
YOU NOTICE THIS TOWN GOT A SLIGHT LEAN TO THE SOUTH?
YUP, FOLLOW THEM FLOOD WATERS AND YOU'LL SEE A FRIENDLY FACE IN NO TIME...
I THINK I SEE SOME FOLKS DOWN THAT AWAY.
D's BOARDIN HOUSE
I AIN'T EVEN GOT TO LOOK. I CAN SMELL IT.
GREEN BEAN CASSEROLE AND CORN BREAD...
TULEY'S KITCHEN
LUNCH
BE SURE TO LET ME DO THE TALKING...

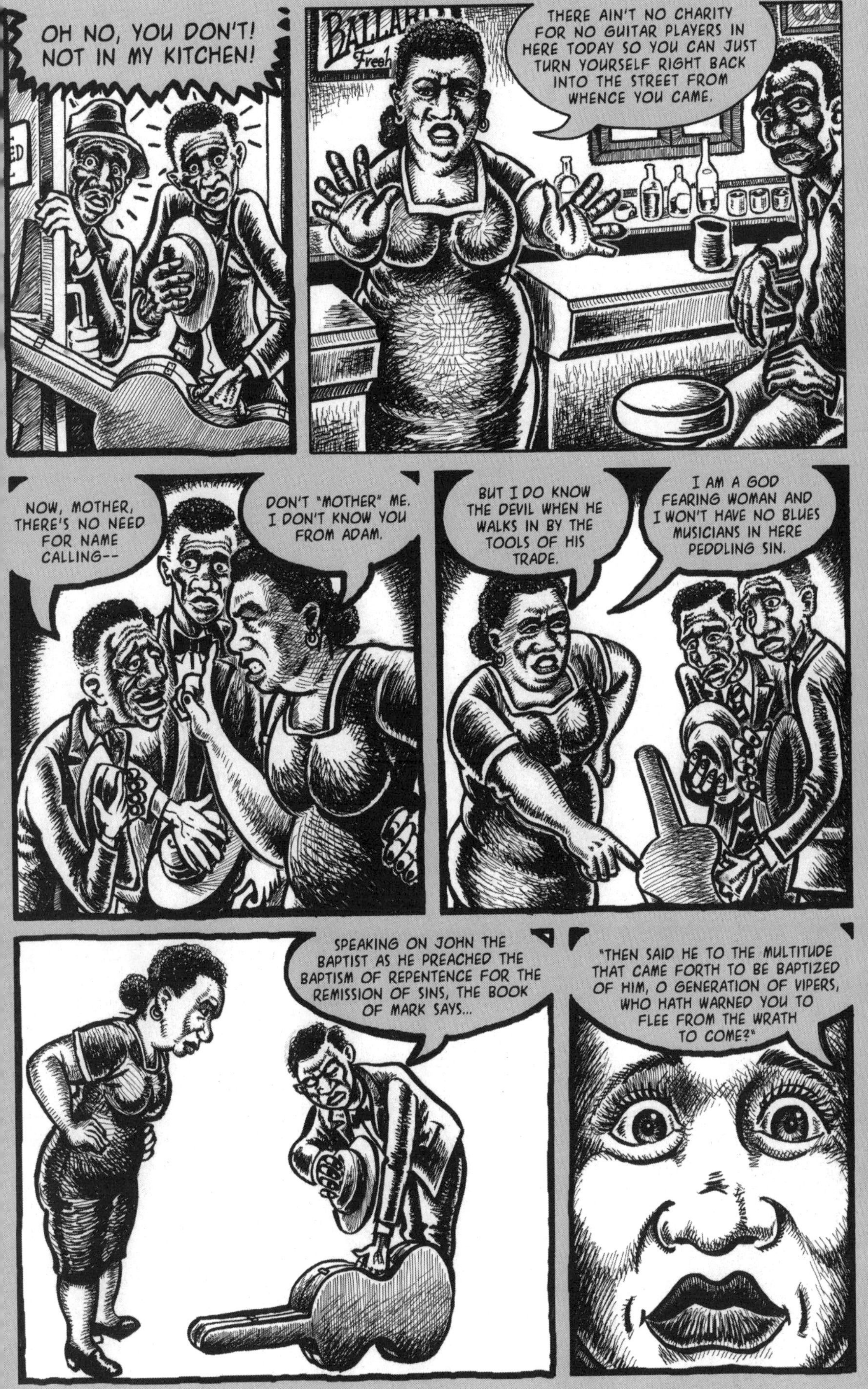
OH NO, YOU DON'T! NOT IN MY KITCHEN!
BALLAR
Fresh
THERE AIN'T NO CHARITY FOR NO GUITAR PLAYERS IN HERE TODAY SO YOU CAN JUST TURN YOURSELF RIGHT BACK INTO THE STREET FROM WHENCE YOU CAME.
NOW, MOTHER, THERE'S NO NEED FOR NAME CALLING--
DON'T "MOTHER" ME. I DON'T KNOW YOU FROM ADAM.
BUT I DO KNOW THE DEVIL WHEN HE WALKS IN BY THE TOOLS OF HIS TRADE.
I AM A GOD FEARING WOMAN AND I WON'T HAVE NO BLUES MUSICIANS IN HERE PEDDLING SIN.
SPEAKING ON JOHN THE BAPTIST AS HE PREACHED THE BAPTISM OF REPENTENCE FOR THE REMISSION OF SINS, THE BOOK OF MARK SAYS...
"THEN SAID HE TO THE MULTITUDE THAT CAME FORTH TO BE BAPTIZED OF HIM, O GENERATION OF VIPERS, WHO HATH WARNED YOU TO FLEE FROM THE WRATH TO COME?"

"BRING FORTH FRUITS WORTHY OF REPENTANCE, AND BEGIN NOT TO SAY WITHIN YOURSELVES, "WE HAVE ABRAHAM AS OUR FATHER" FOR I SAY UNTO YOU THAT GOD IS ABLE OF THESE STONES TO RAISE UP CHILDREN UNTO ABRAHAM".

"AND NOW ALSO THE AXE IS LAID UNTO THE ROOT OF THE TREES: EVERY TREE THEREFORE WHICH BRINGETH NOT FORTH GOOD FRUIT IS HEWN DOWN...

...AND CAST INTO THE FIRE".

SWEET JESUS...

AND THE PEOPLE ASKED HIM, SAYING, "WHAT SHALL WE DO THEN?"

"HE ANSWERETH AND SAITH UNTO THEM, HE THAT HATH TWO COATS, LET HIM IMPART THEM TO HIM THAT HATH NONE...

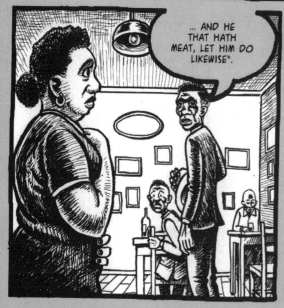

... AND HE THAT HATH MEAT, LET HIM DO LIKEWISE".

... AMEN.

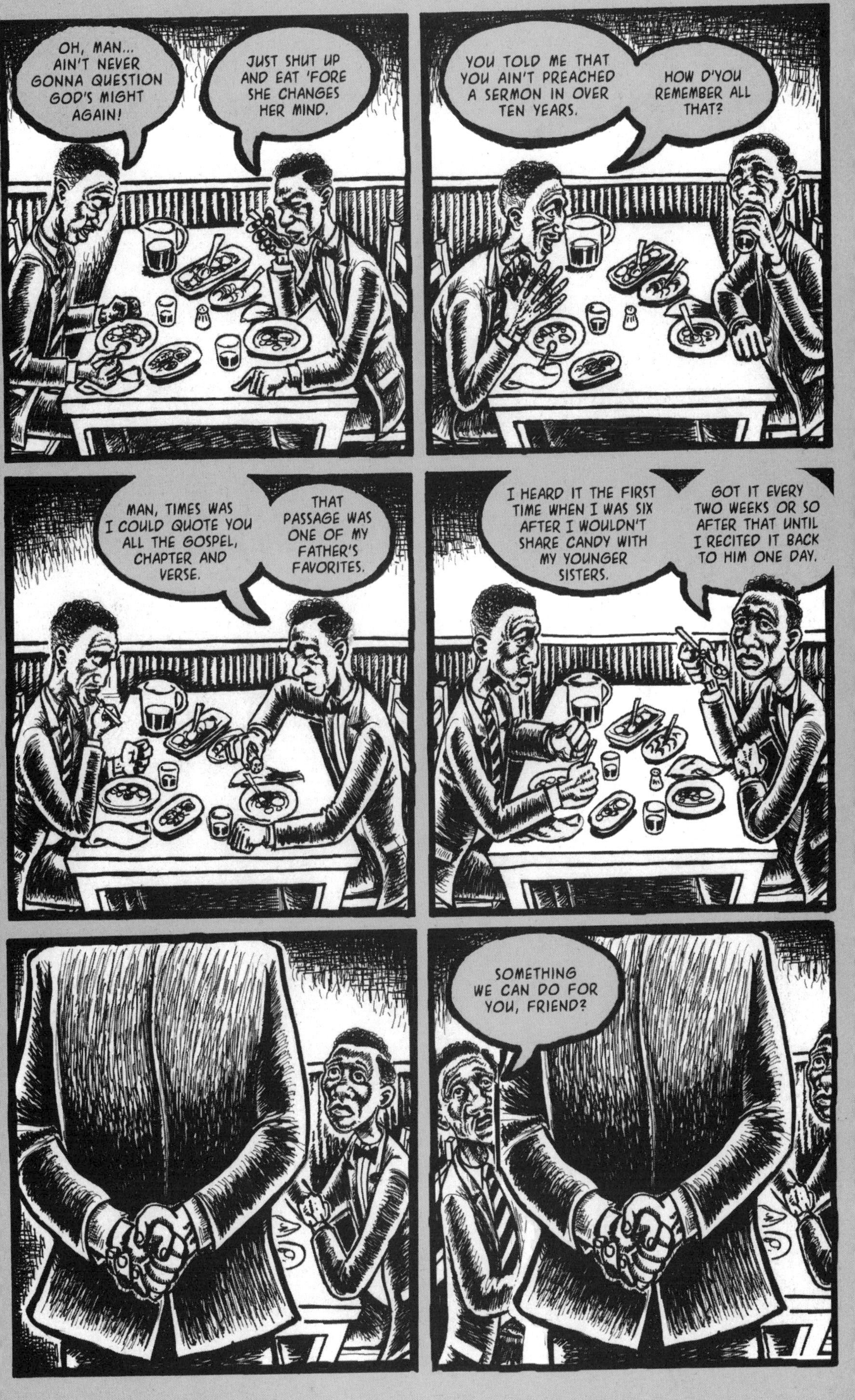

OH, MAN... AIN'T NEVER GONNA QUESTION GOD'S MIGHT AGAIN!
JUST SHUT UP AND EAT 'FORE SHE CHANGES HER MIND.
YOU TOLD ME THAT YOU AIN'T PREACHED A SERMON IN OVER TEN YEARS.
HOW D'YOU REMEMBER ALL THAT?
MAN, TIMES WAS I COULD QUOTE YOU ALL THE GOSPEL, CHAPTER AND VERSE.
THAT PASSAGE WAS ONE OF MY FATHER'S FAVORITES.
I HEARD IT THE FIRST TIME WHEN I WAS SIX AFTER I WOULDN'T SHARE CANDY WITH MY YOUNGER SISTERS.
GOT IT EVERY TWO WEEKS OR SO AFTER THAT UNTIL I RECITED IT BACK TO HIM ONE DAY.
SOMETHING WE CAN DO FOR YOU, FRIEND?

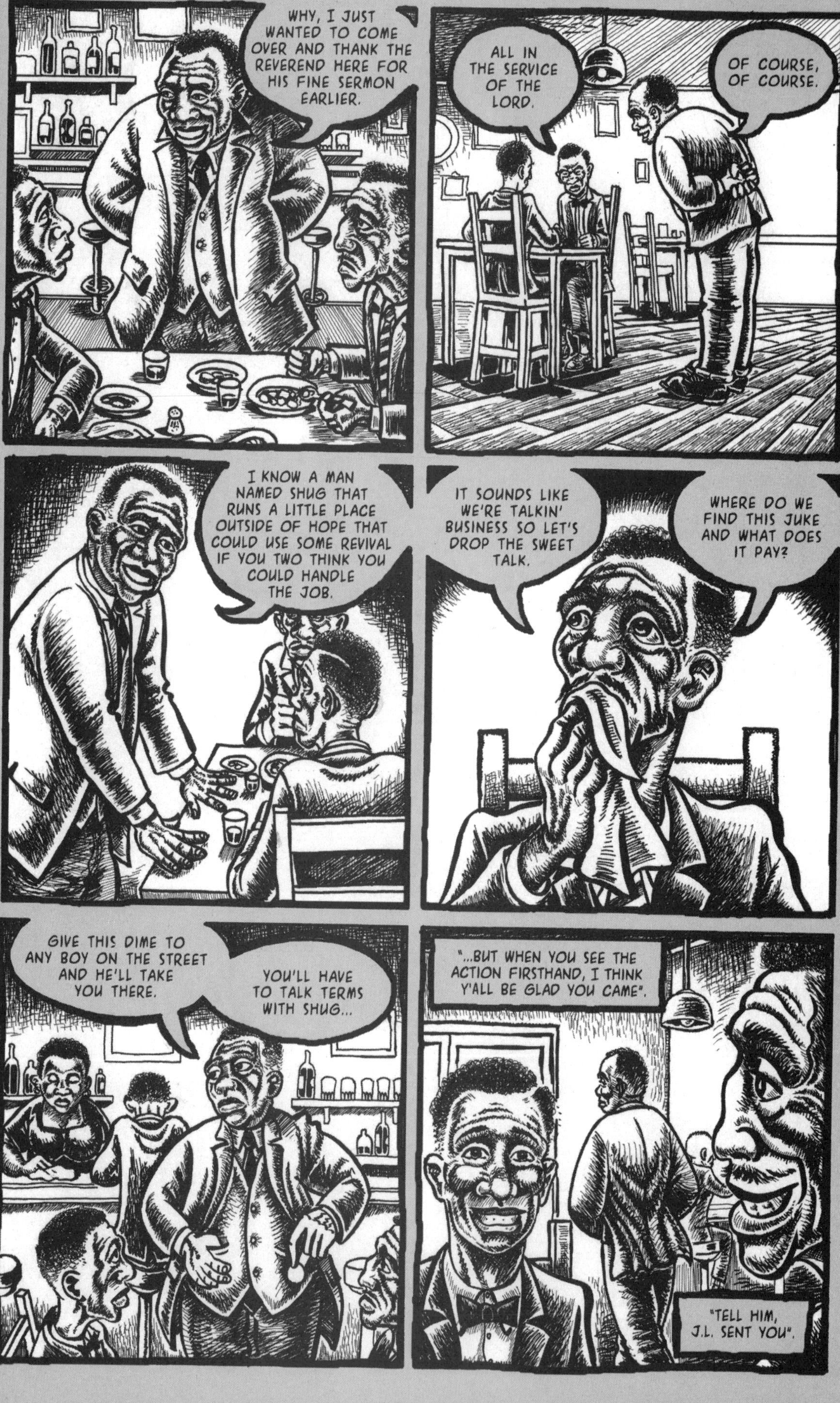
WHY, I JUST WANTED TO COME OVER AND THANK THE REVEREND HERE FOR HIS FINE SERMON EARLIER.
ALL IN THE SERVICE OF THE LORD.
OF COURSE, OF COURSE.
I KNOW A MAN NAMED SHUG THAT RUNS A LITTLE PLACE OUTSIDE OF HOPE THAT COULD USE SOME REVIVAL IF YOU TWO THINK YOU COULD HANDLE THE JOB.
IT SOUNDS LIKE WE'RE TALKIN' BUSINESS SO LET'S DROP THE SWEET TALK.
WHERE DO WE FIND THIS JUKE AND WHAT DOES IT PAY?
GIVE THIS DIME TO ANY BOY ON THE STREET AND HE'LL TAKE YOU THERE.
YOU'LL HAVE TO TALK TERMS WITH SHUG...
"...BUT WHEN YOU SEE THE ACTION FIRSTHAND, I THINK Y'ALL BE GLAD YOU CAME".
"TELL HIM, J.L. SENT YOU".

2

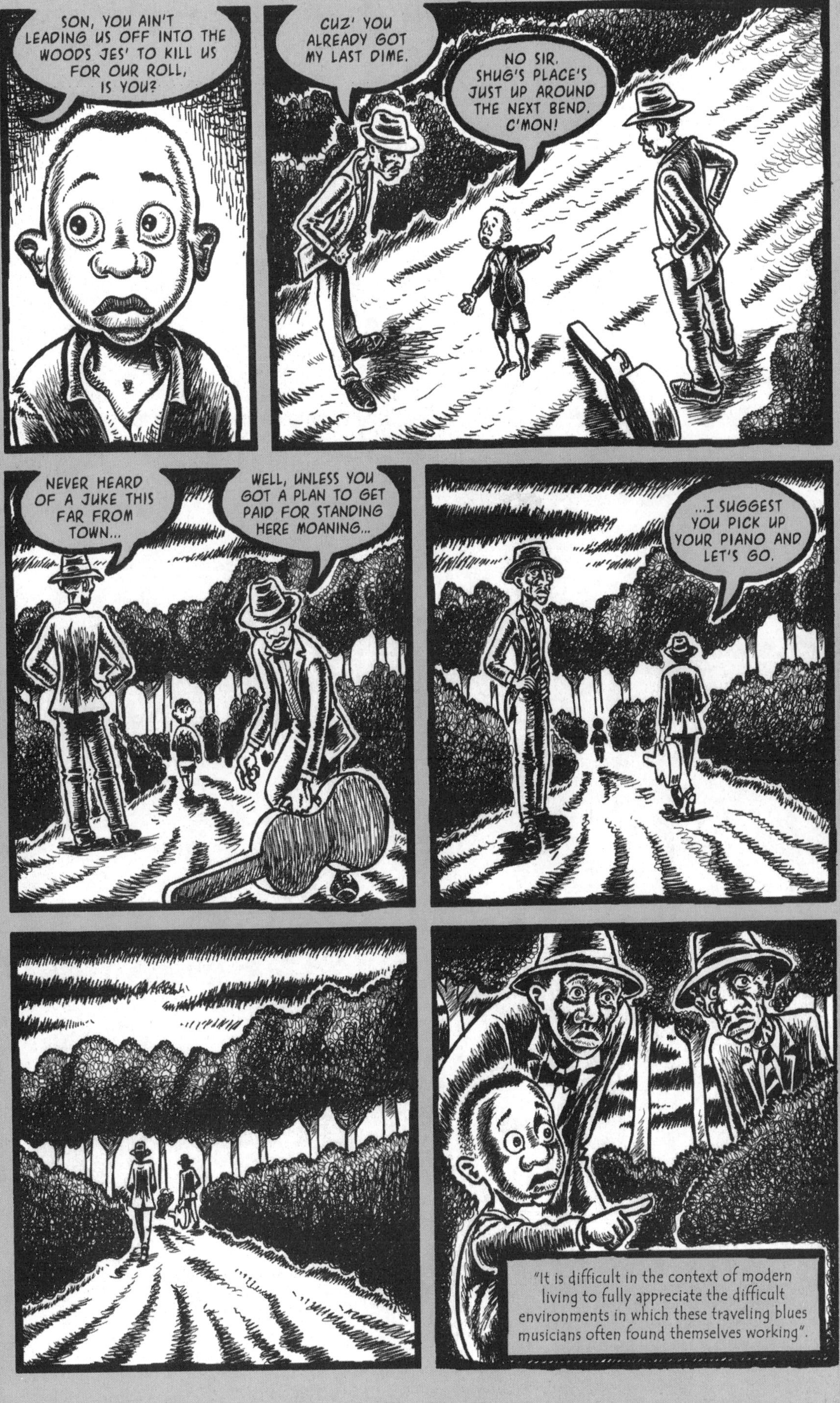
SON, YOU AIN'T LEADING US OFF INTO THE WOODS JES' TO KILL US FOR OUR ROLL, IS YOU?
CUZ' YOU ALREADY GOT MY LAST DIME.
NO SIR. SHUG'S PLACE'S JUST UP AROUND THE NEXT BEND. C'MON!
NEVER HEARD OF A JUKE THIS FAR FROM TOWN...
WELL, UNLESS YOU GOT A PLAN TO GET PAID FOR STANDING HERE MOANING...
...I SUGGEST YOU PICK UP YOUR PIANO AND LET'S GO.
"It is difficult in the context of modern living to fully appreciate the difficult environments in which these traveling blues musicians often found themselves working".

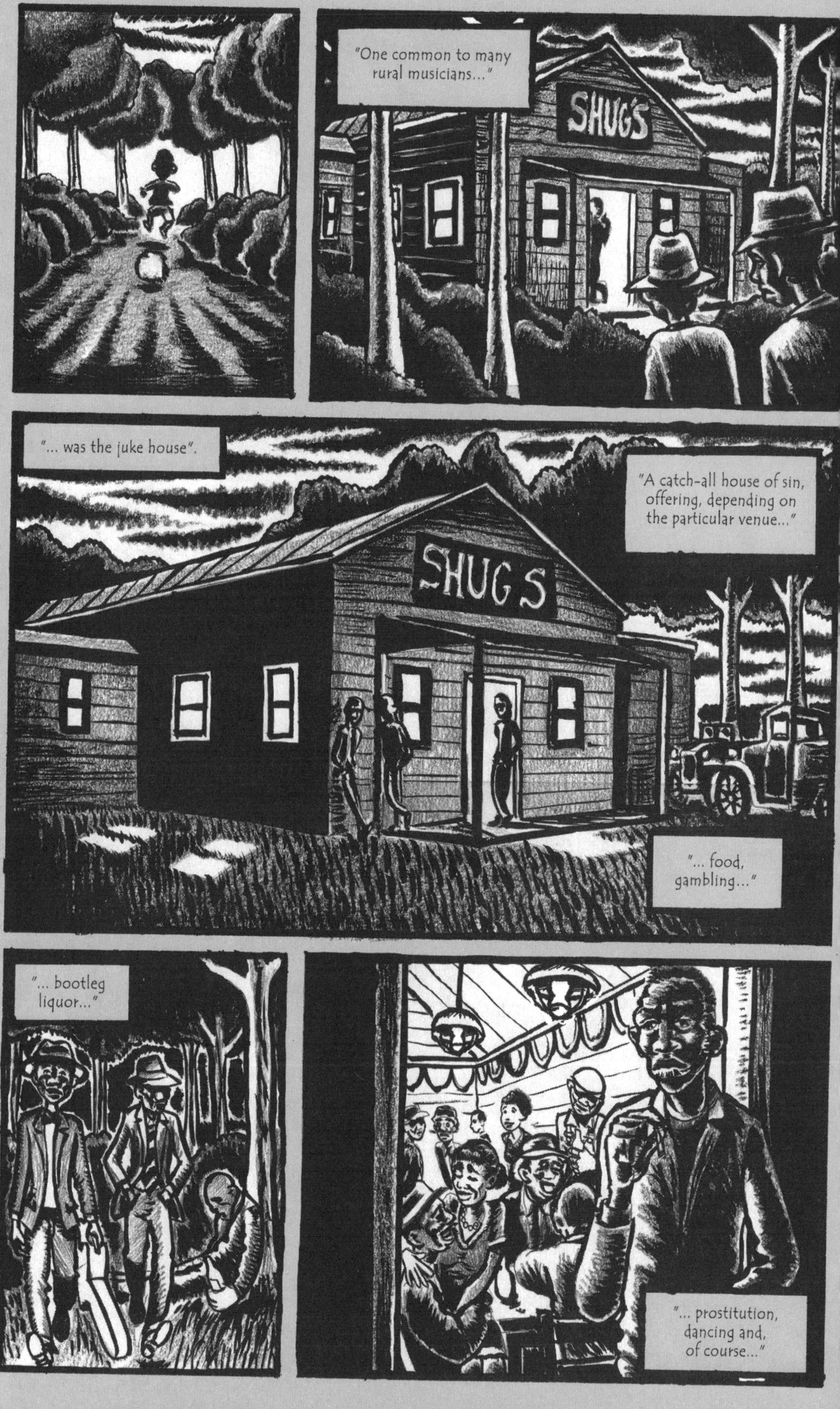
"One common to many rural musicians..."
SHUG'S
"... was the juke house".
"A catch-all house of sin, offering, depending on the particular venue..."
SHUG'S
"... food, gambling..."
"... bootleg liquor..."
"... prostitution, dancing and, of course..."

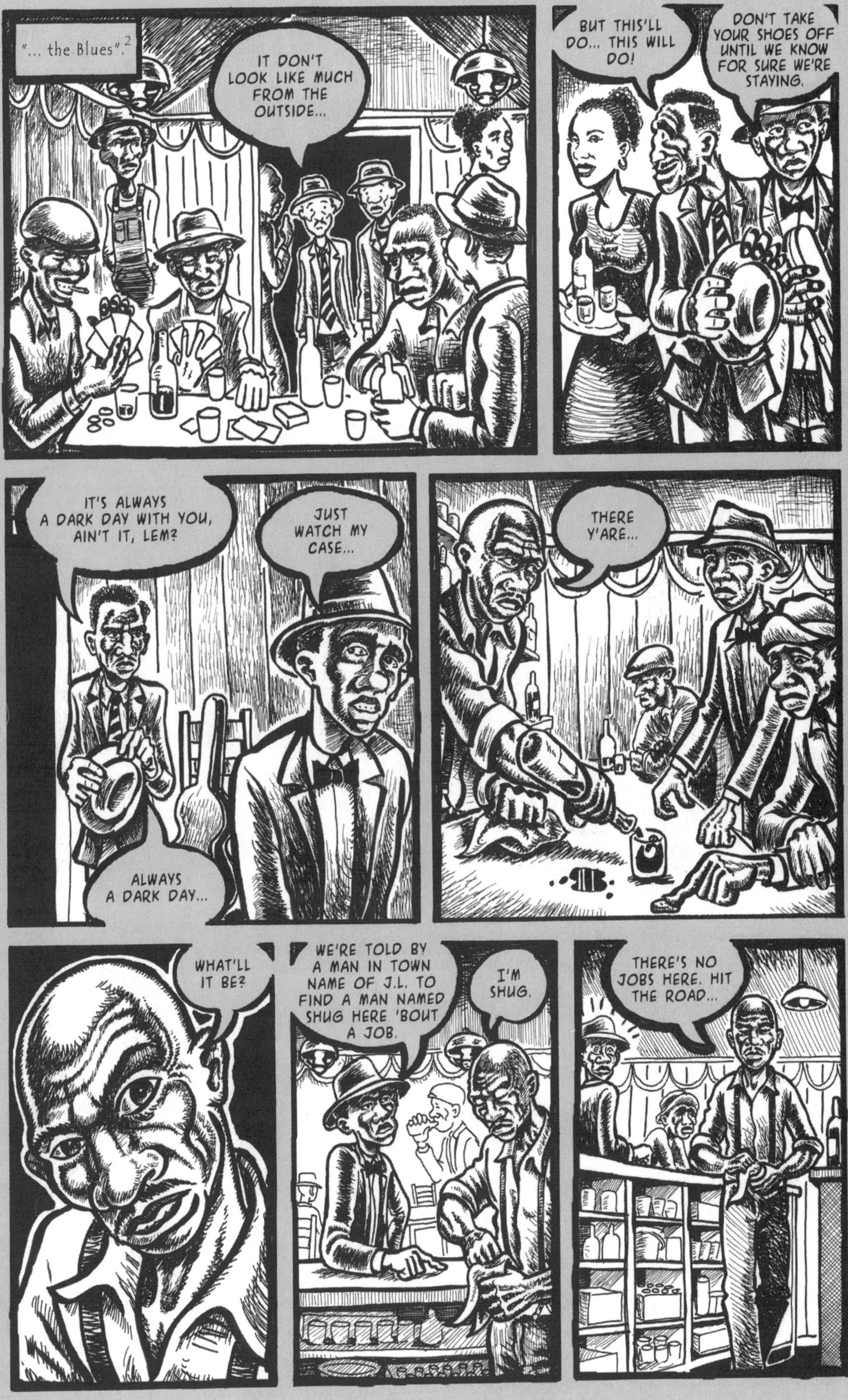
"... the Blues".[2]
IT DON'T LOOK LIKE MUCH FROM THE OUTSIDE...
BUT THIS'LL DO... THIS WILL DO!
DON'T TAKE YOUR SHOES OFF UNTIL WE KNOW FOR SURE WE'RE STAYING.
IT'S ALWAYS A DARK DAY WITH YOU, AIN'T IT, LEM?
JUST WATCH MY CASE...
ALWAYS A DARK DAY...
THERE Y'ARE...
WHAT'LL IT BE?
WE'RE TOLD BY A MAN IN TOWN NAME OF J.L. TO FIND A MAN NAMED SHUG HERE 'BOUT A JOB.
I'M SHUG.
THERE'S NO JOBS HERE. HIT THE ROAD...

[2] Deldoff, ibid.

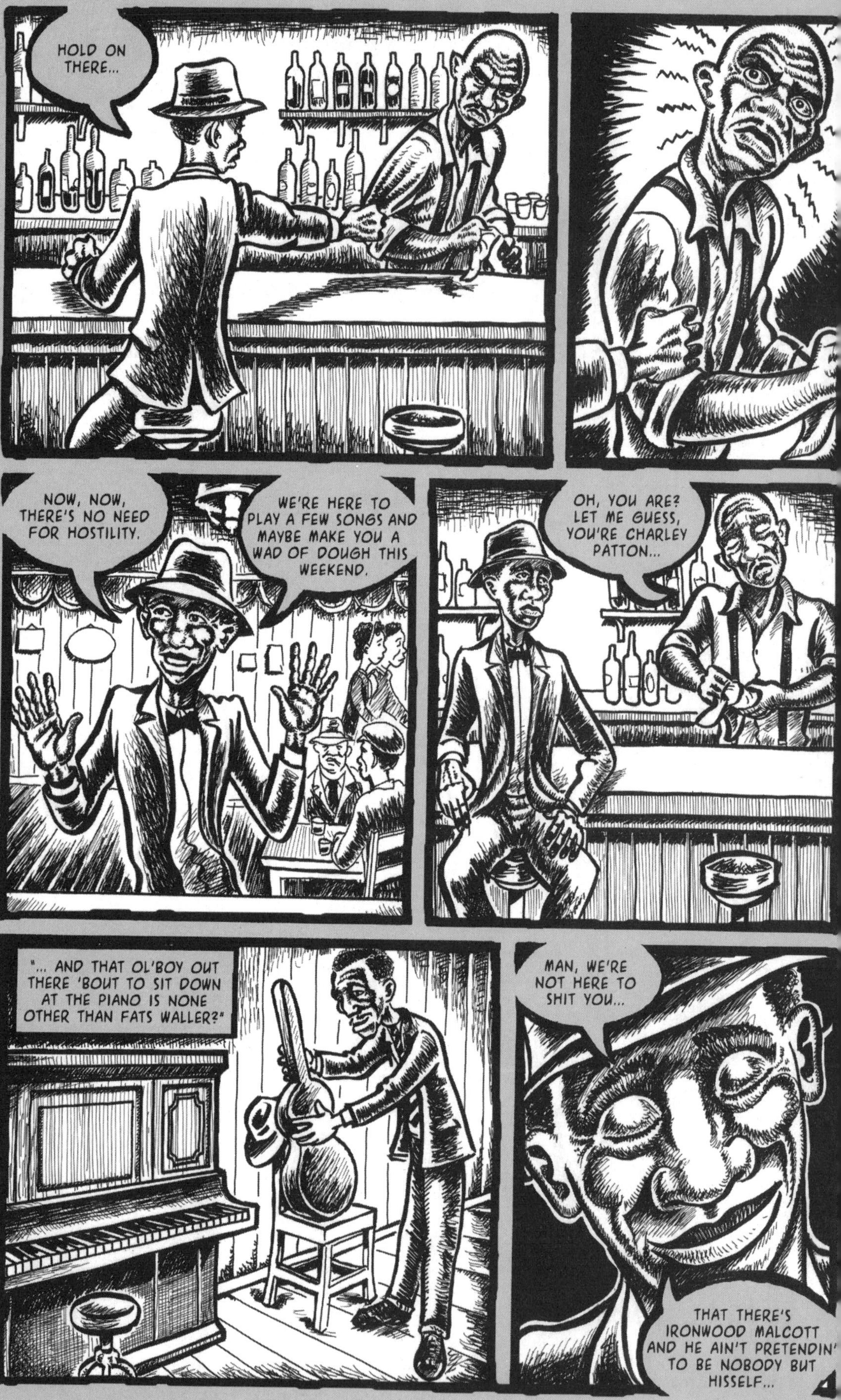
HOLD ON THERE...
NOW, NOW, THERE'S NO NEED FOR HOSTILITY.
WE'RE HERE TO PLAY A FEW SONGS AND MAYBE MAKE YOU A WAD OF DOUGH THIS WEEKEND.
OH, YOU ARE? LET ME GUESS, YOU'RE CHARLEY PATTON...
"... AND THAT OL'BOY OUT THERE 'BOUT TO SIT DOWN AT THE PIANO IS NONE OTHER THAN FATS WALLER?"
MAN, WE'RE NOT HERE TO SHIT YOU...
THAT THERE'S IRONWOOD MALCOTT AND HE AIN'T PRETENDIN' TO BE NOBODY BUT HISSELF...
4

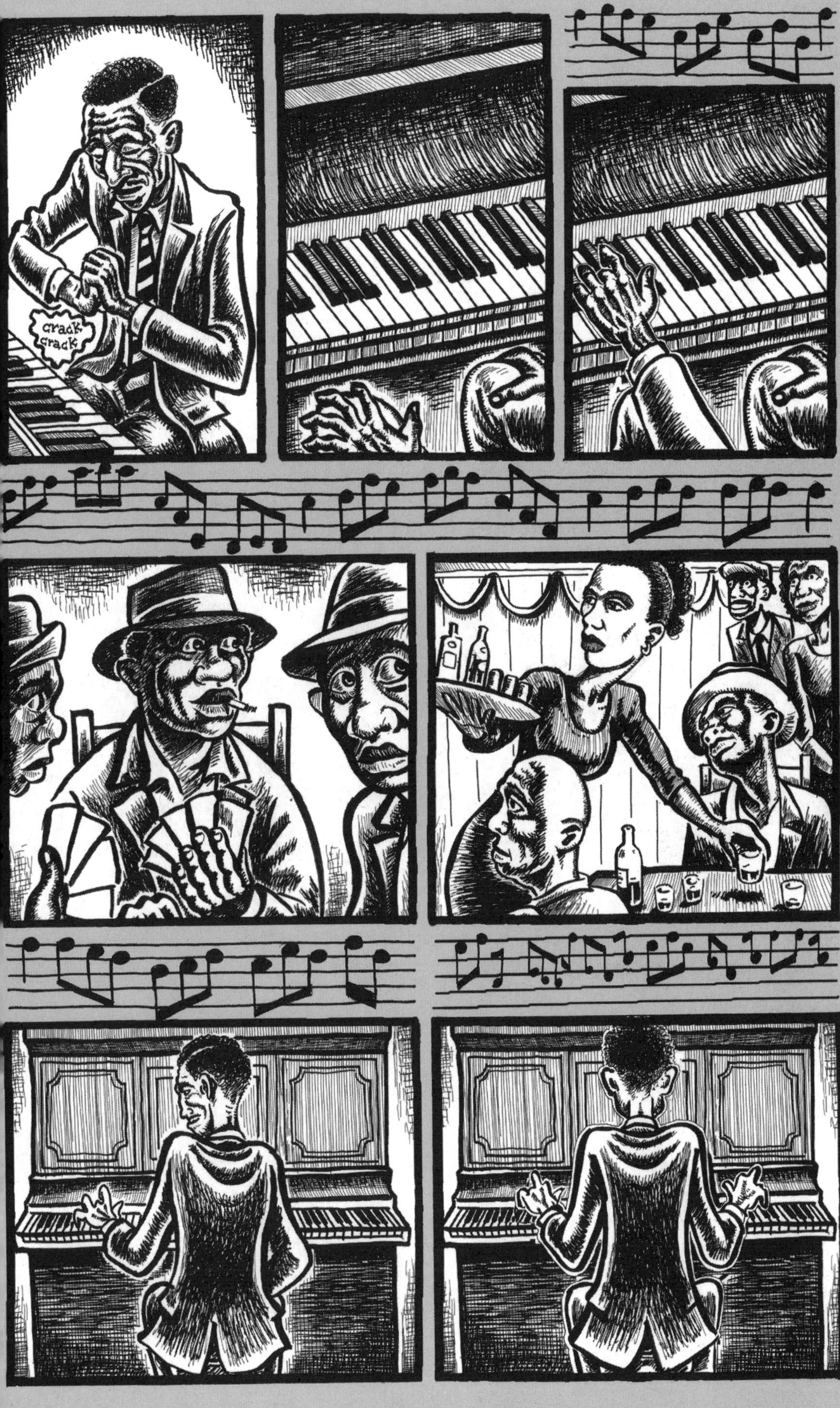
crack
crack

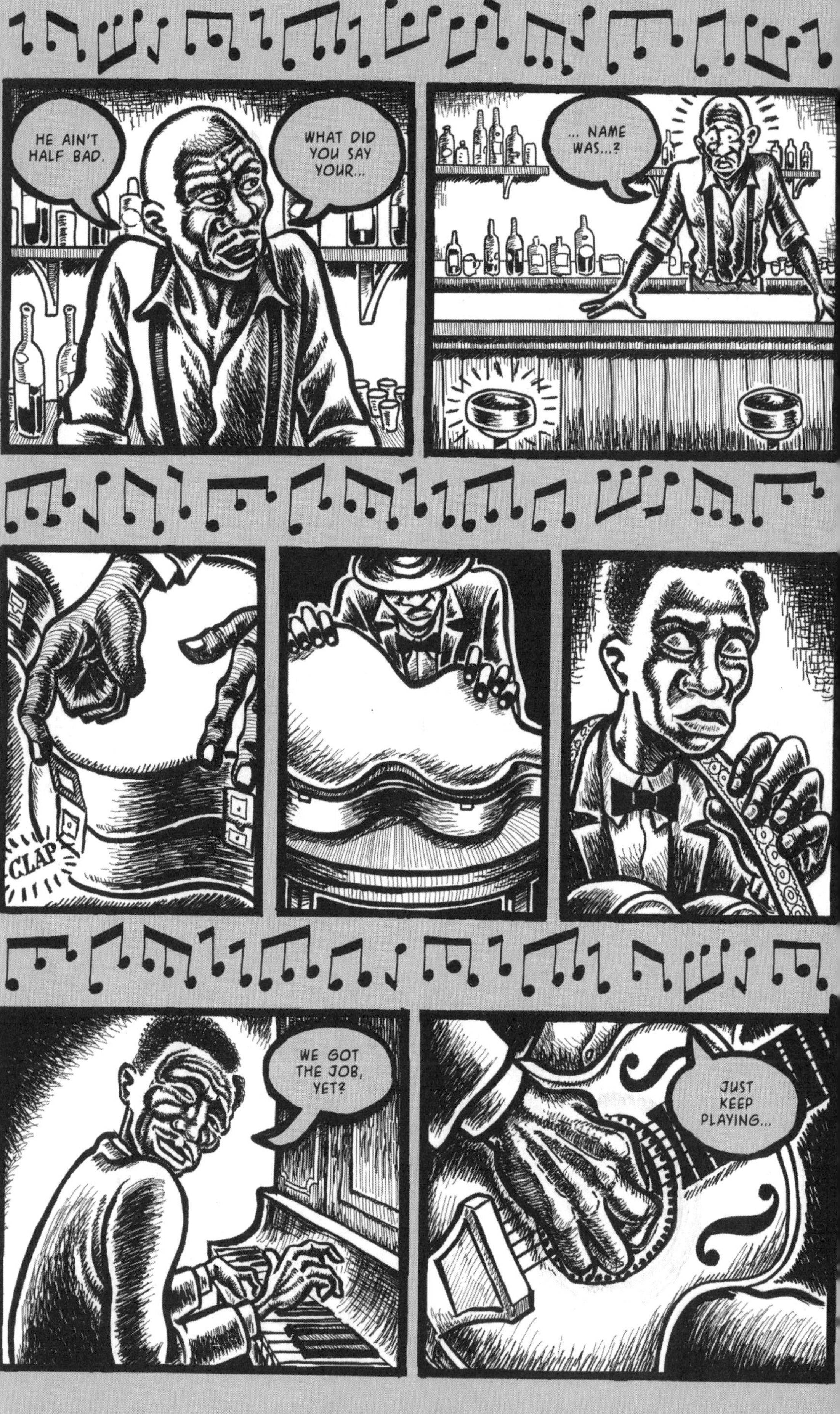
HE AIN'T HALF BAD.
WHAT DID YOU SAY YOUR...
... NAME WAS...?
CLAP
WE GOT THE JOB, YET?
JUST KEEP PLAYING...

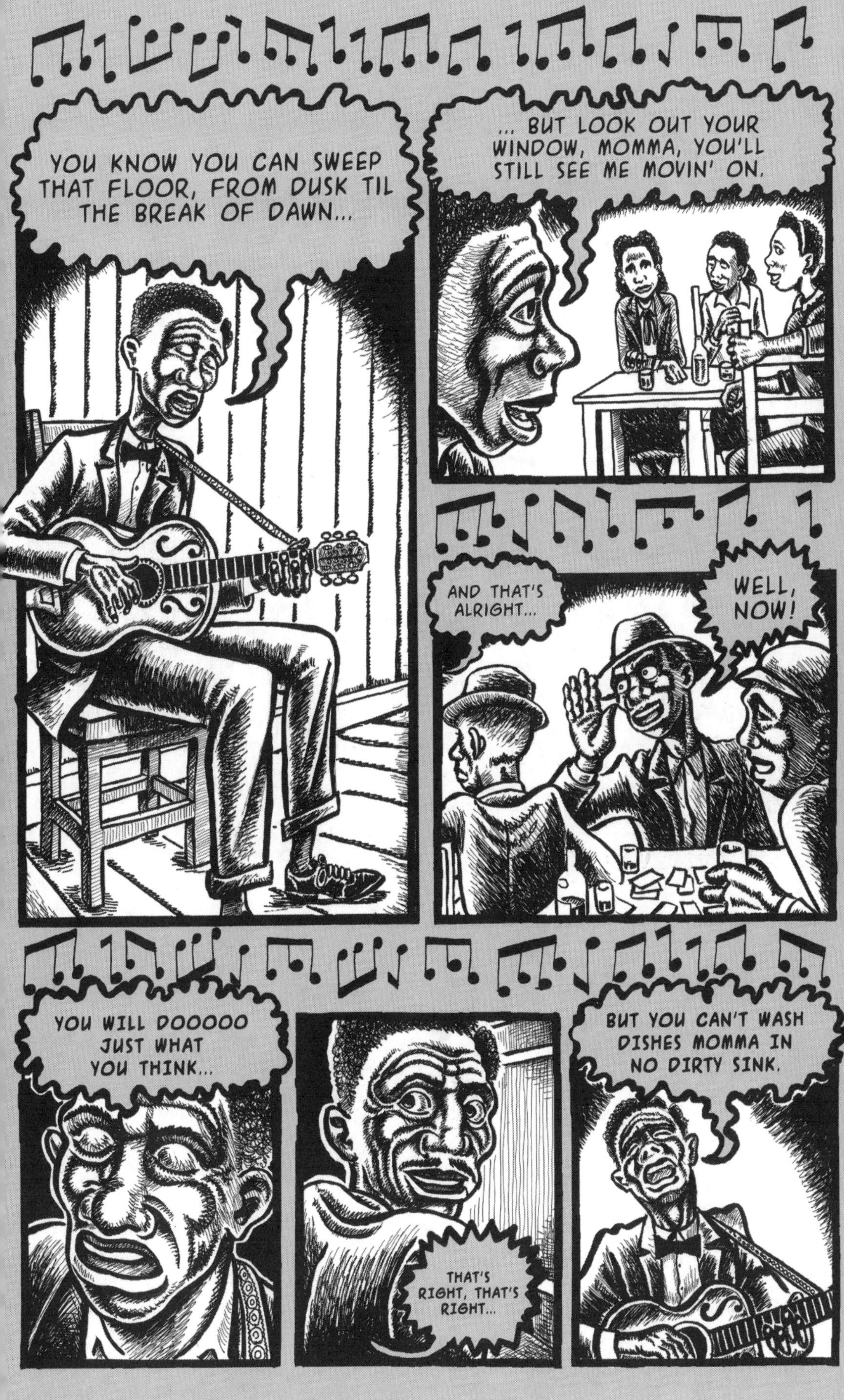
YOU KNOW YOU CAN SWEEP THAT FLOOR, FROM DUSK TIL THE BREAK OF DAWN...
... BUT LOOK OUT YOUR WINDOW, MOMMA, YOU'LL STILL SEE ME MOVIN' ON.
AND THAT'S ALRIGHT...
WELL, NOW!
YOU WILL DOOOOO JUST WHAT YOU THINK...
THAT'S RIGHT, THAT'S RIGHT...
BUT YOU CAN'T WASH DISHES MOMMA IN NO DIRTY SINK.

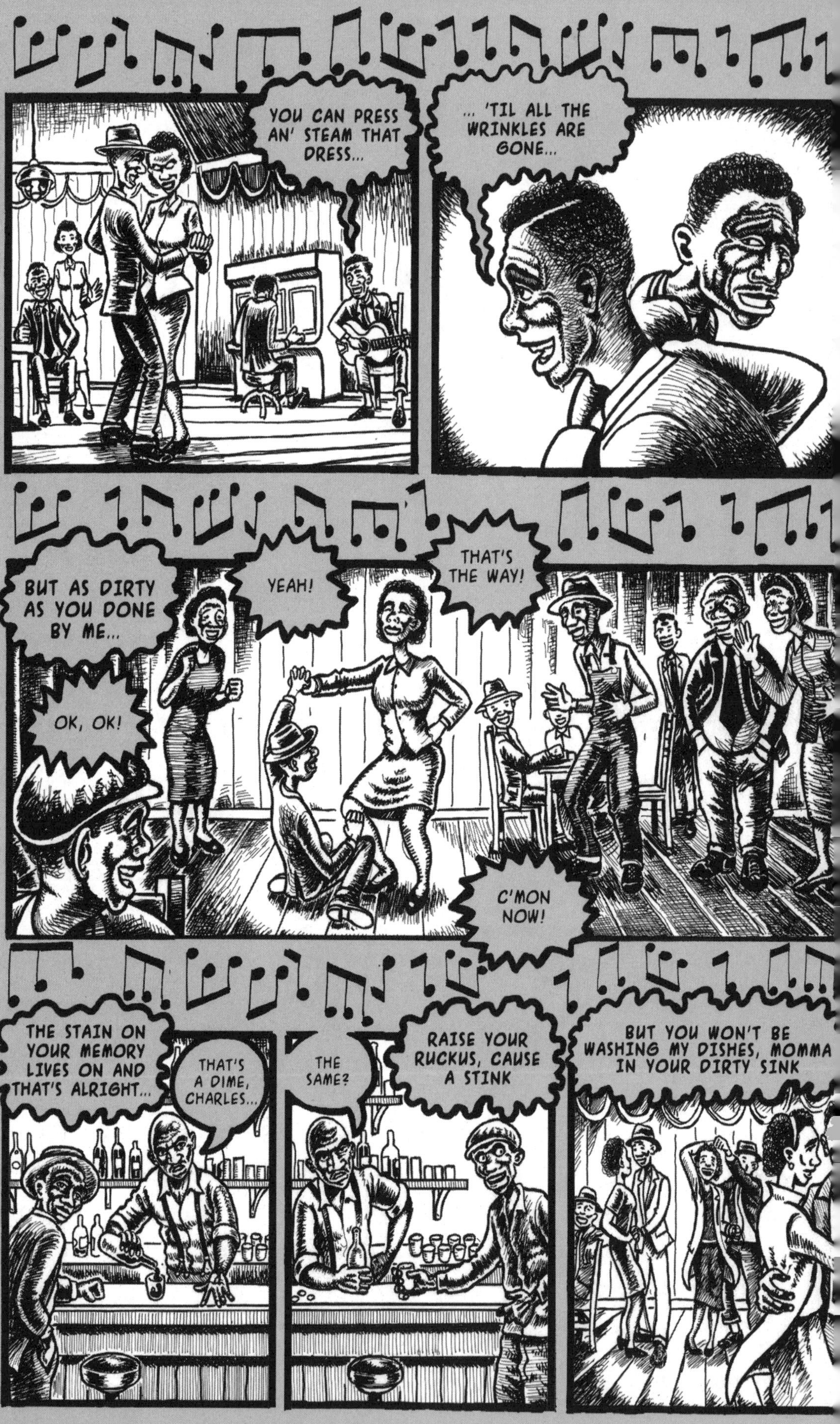
YOU CAN PRESS AN' STEAM THAT DRESS...
... 'TIL ALL THE WRINKLES ARE GONE...
BUT AS DIRTY AS YOU DONE BY ME...
YEAH!
THAT'S THE WAY!
OK, OK!
C'MON NOW!
THE STAIN ON YOUR MEMORY LIVES ON AND THAT'S ALRIGHT...
THAT'S A DIME, CHARLES...
THE SAME?
RAISE YOUR RUCKUS, CAUSE A STINK
BUT YOU WON'T BE WASHING MY DISHES, MOMMA IN YOUR DIRTY SINK

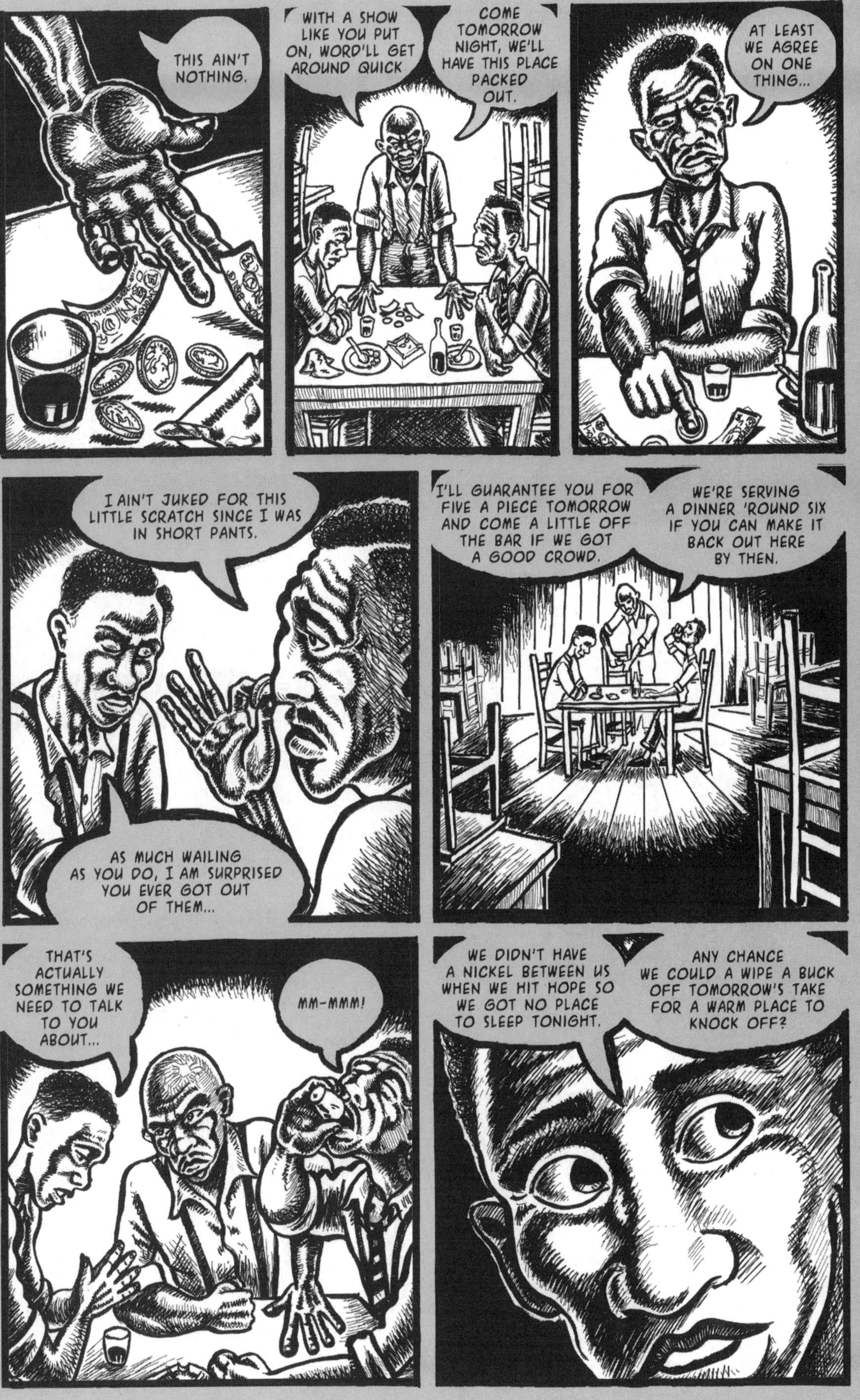
THIS AIN'T NOTHING.
WITH A SHOW LIKE YOU PUT ON, WORD'LL GET AROUND QUICK
COME TOMORROW NIGHT, WE'LL HAVE THIS PLACE PACKED OUT.
AT LEAST WE AGREE ON ONE THING...
I AIN'T JUKED FOR THIS LITTLE SCRATCH SINCE I WAS IN SHORT PANTS.
AS MUCH WAILING AS YOU DO, I AM SURPRISED YOU EVER GOT OUT OF THEM...
I'LL GUARANTEE YOU FOR FIVE A PIECE TOMORROW AND COME A LITTLE OFF THE BAR IF WE GOT A GOOD CROWD.
WE'RE SERVING A DINNER 'ROUND SIX IF YOU CAN MAKE IT BACK OUT HERE BY THEN.
THAT'S ACTUALLY SOMETHING WE NEED TO TALK TO YOU ABOUT...
MM-MMM!
WE DIDN'T HAVE A NICKEL BETWEEN US WHEN WE HIT HOPE SO WE GOT NO PLACE TO SLEEP TONIGHT.
ANY CHANCE WE COULD A WIPE A BUCK OFF TOMORROW'S TAKE FOR A WARM PLACE TO KNOCK OFF?

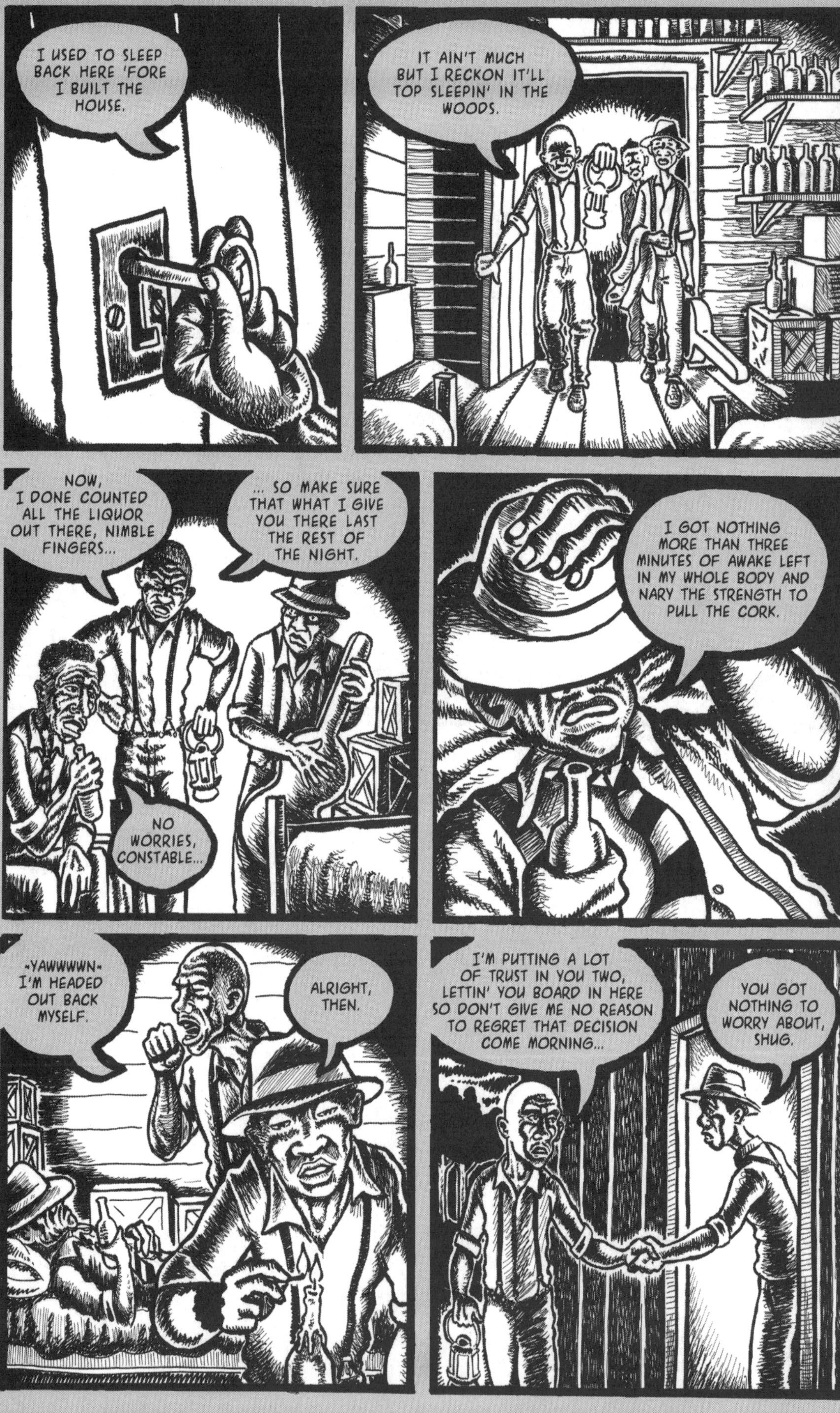
I USED TO SLEEP BACK HERE 'FORE I BUILT THE HOUSE.
IT AIN'T MUCH BUT I RECKON IT'LL TOP SLEEPIN' IN THE WOODS.
NOW, I DONE COUNTED ALL THE LIQUOR OUT THERE, NIMBLE FINGERS...
... SO MAKE SURE THAT WHAT I GIVE YOU THERE LAST THE REST OF THE NIGHT.
NO WORRIES, CONSTABLE...
I GOT NOTHING MORE THAN THREE MINUTES OF AWAKE LEFT IN MY WHOLE BODY AND NARY THE STRENGTH TO PULL THE CORK.
«YAWWWWN» I'M HEADED OUT BACK MYSELF.
ALRIGHT, THEN.
I'M PUTTING A LOT OF TRUST IN YOU TWO, LETTIN' YOU BOARD IN HERE SO DON'T GIVE ME NO REASON TO REGRET THAT DECISION COME MORNING...
YOU GOT NOTHING TO WORRY ABOUT, SHUG.

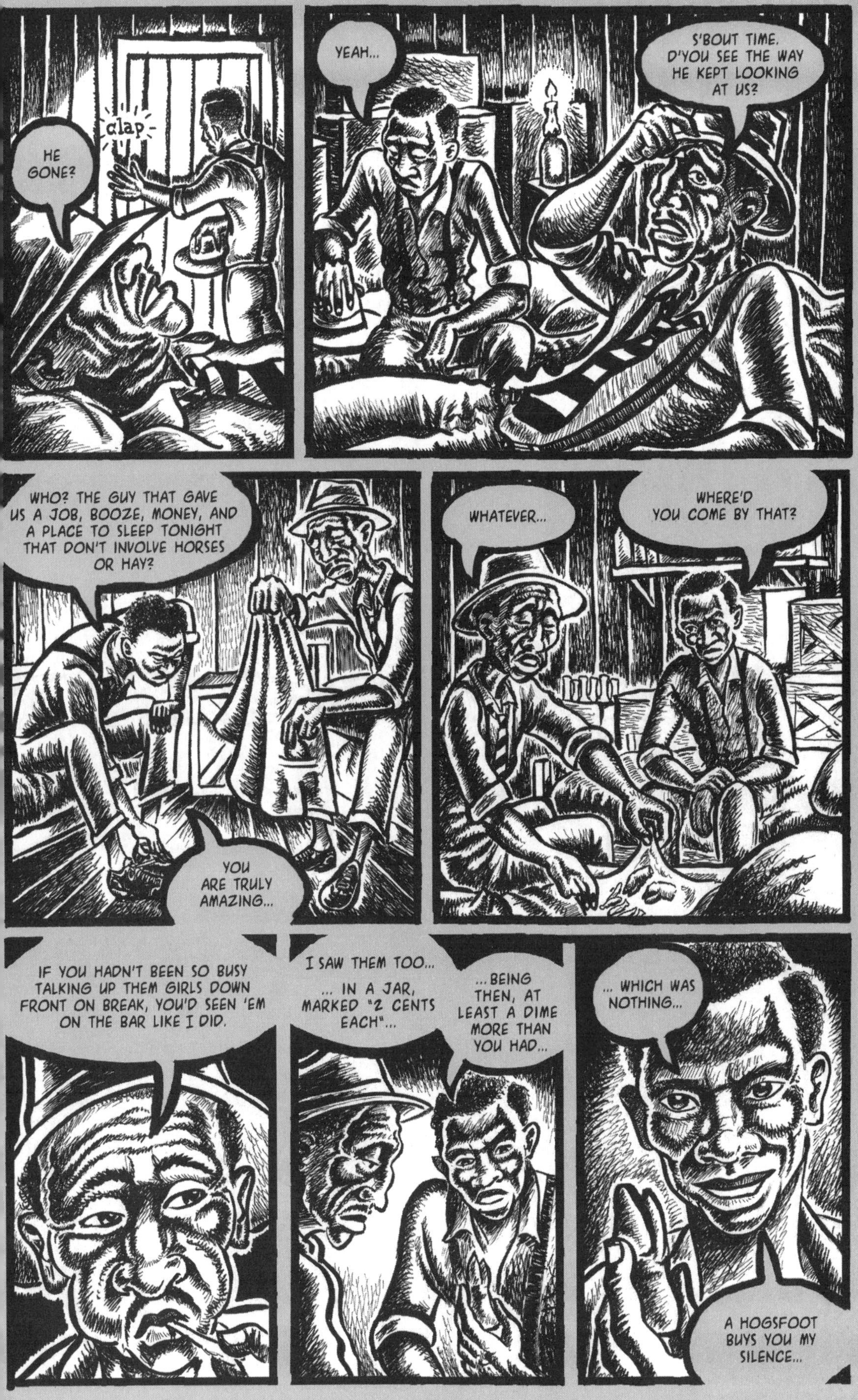
HE GONE?
clap
YEAH...
S'BOUT TIME. D'YOU SEE THE WAY HE KEPT LOOKING AT US?
WHO? THE GUY THAT GAVE US A JOB, BOOZE, MONEY, AND A PLACE TO SLEEP TONIGHT THAT DON'T INVOLVE HORSES OR HAY?
YOU ARE TRULY AMAZING...
WHATEVER...
WHERE'D YOU COME BY THAT?
IF YOU HADN'T BEEN SO BUSY TALKING UP THEM GIRLS DOWN FRONT ON BREAK, YOU'D SEEN 'EM ON THE BAR LIKE I DID.
I SAW THEM TOO...
... IN A JAR, MARKED "2 CENTS EACH"...
...BEING THEN, AT LEAST A DIME MORE THAN YOU HAD...
... WHICH WAS NOTHING...
A HOGSFOOT BUYS YOU MY SILENCE...

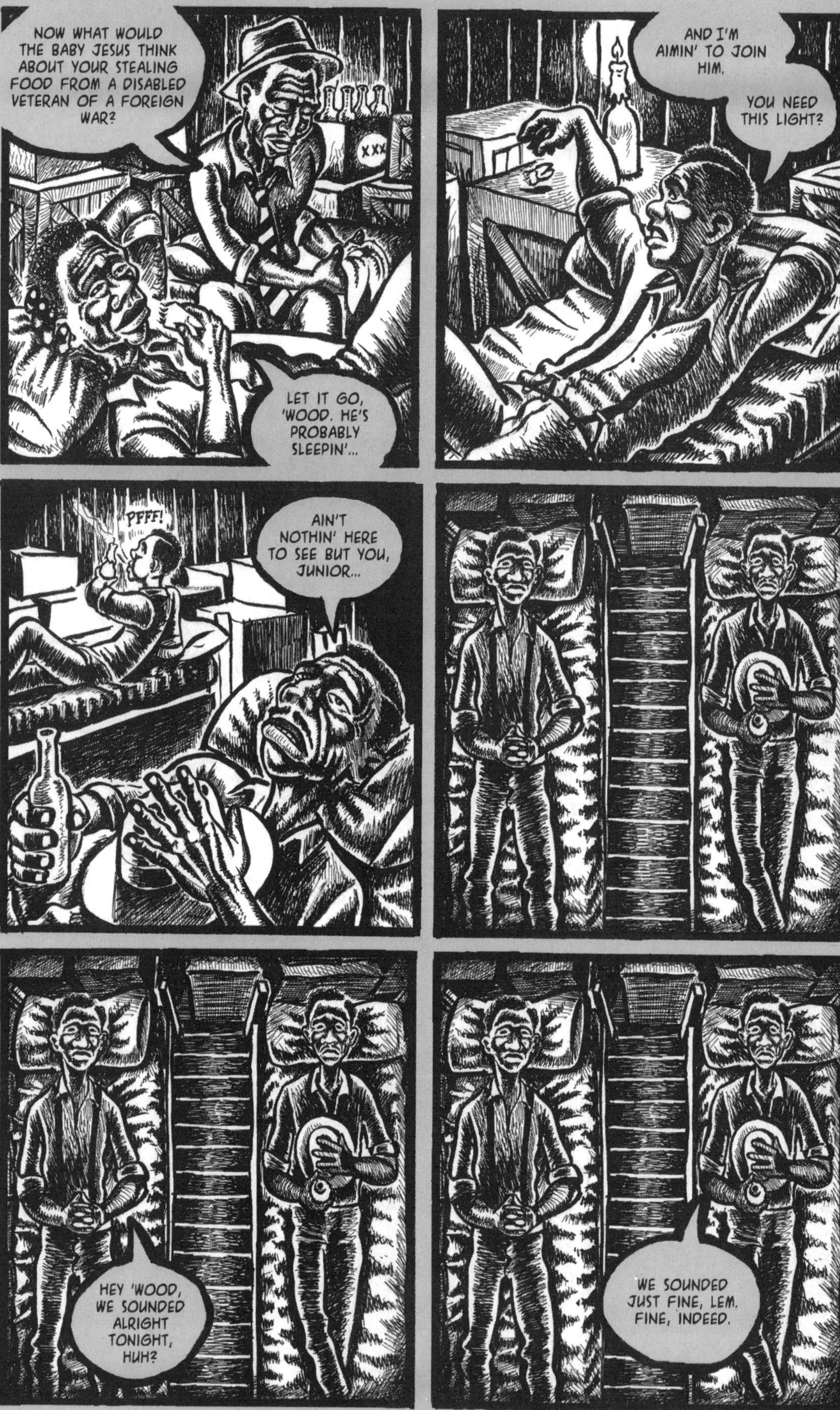
NOW WHAT WOULD THE BABY JESUS THINK ABOUT YOUR STEALING FOOD FROM A DISABLED VETERAN OF A FOREIGN WAR?
LET IT GO, 'WOOD. HE'S PROBABLY SLEEPIN'...
AND I'M AIMIN' TO JOIN HIM.
YOU NEED THIS LIGHT?
PFFF!
AIN'T NOTHIN' HERE TO SEE BUT YOU, JUNIOR...
HEY 'WOOD, WE SOUNDED ALRIGHT TONIGHT, HUH?
WE SOUNDED JUST FINE, LEM. FINE, INDEED.

3

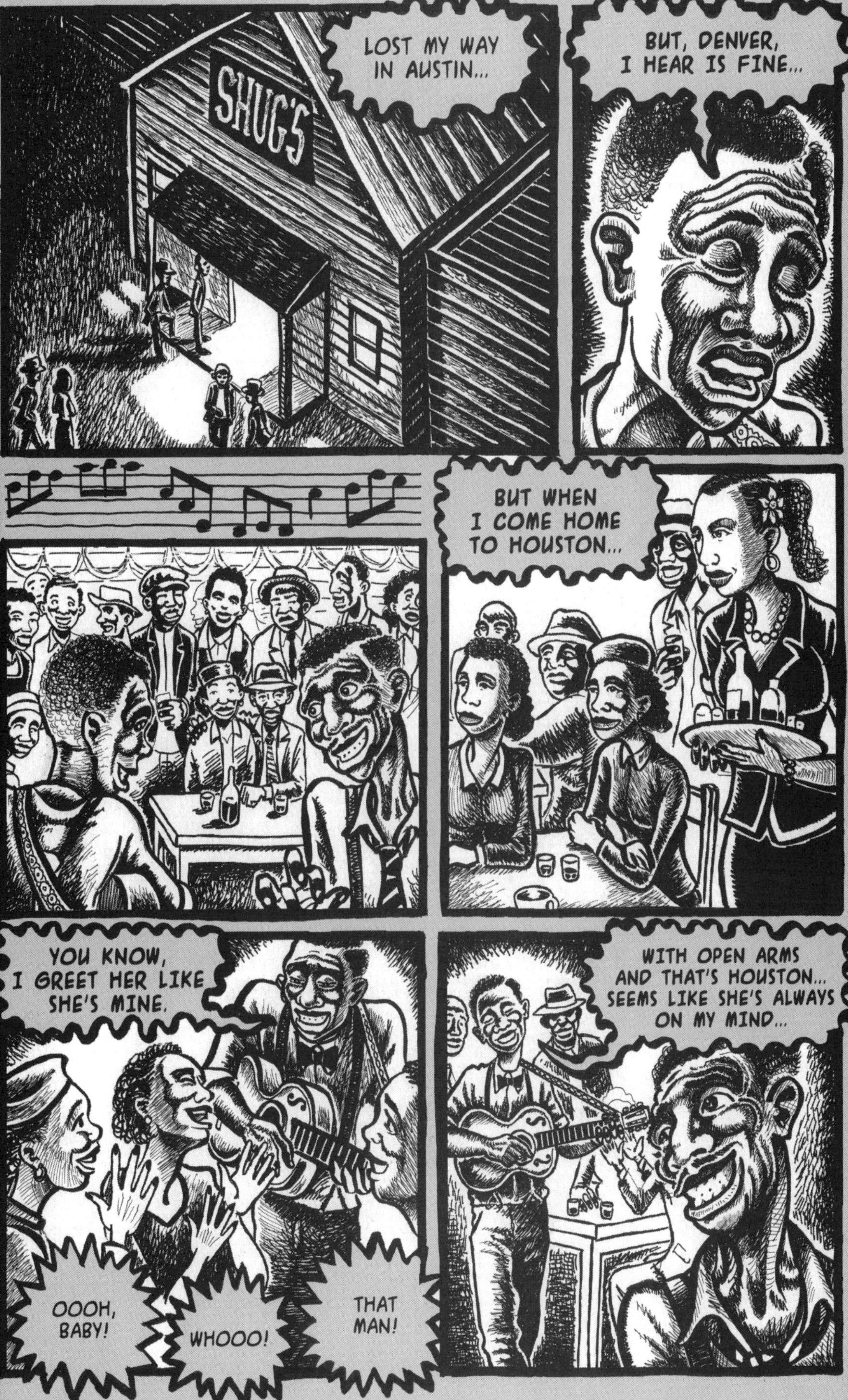
SHUG'S
LOST MY WAY IN AUSTIN...
BUT, DENVER, I HEAR IS FINE...
BUT WHEN I COME HOME TO HOUSTON...
YOU KNOW, I GREET HER LIKE SHE'S MINE.
OOOH, BABY!
WHOOO!
THAT MAN!
WITH OPEN ARMS AND THAT'S HOUSTON... SEEMS LIKE SHE'S ALWAYS ON MY MIND...

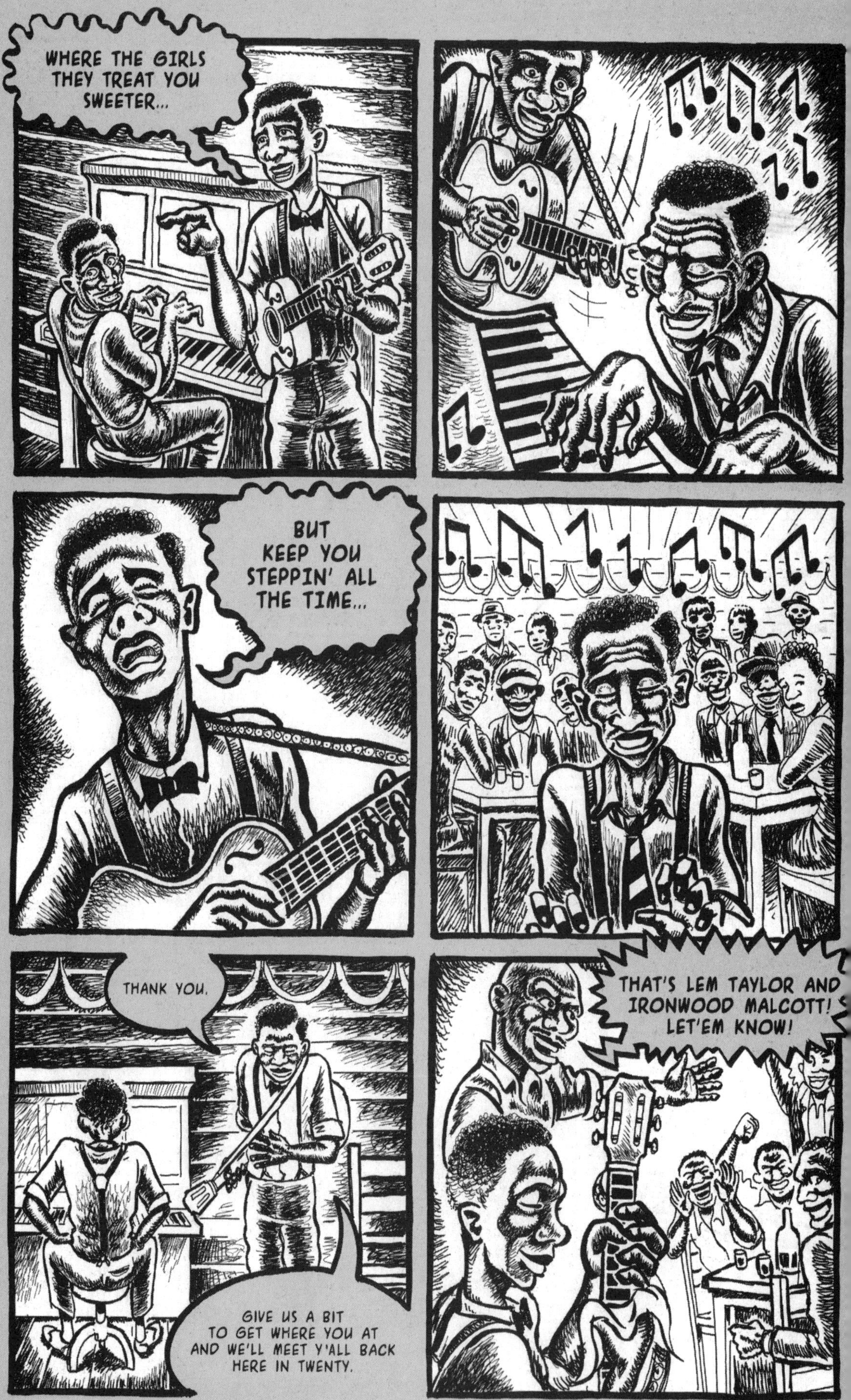
WHERE THE GIRLS THEY TREAT YOU SWEETER...
BUT KEEP YOU STEPPIN' ALL THE TIME...
THANK YOU.
GIVE US A BIT TO GET WHERE YOU AT AND WE'LL MEET Y'ALL BACK HERE IN TWENTY.
THAT'S LEM TAYLOR AND IRONWOOD MALCOTT! LET'EM KNOW!

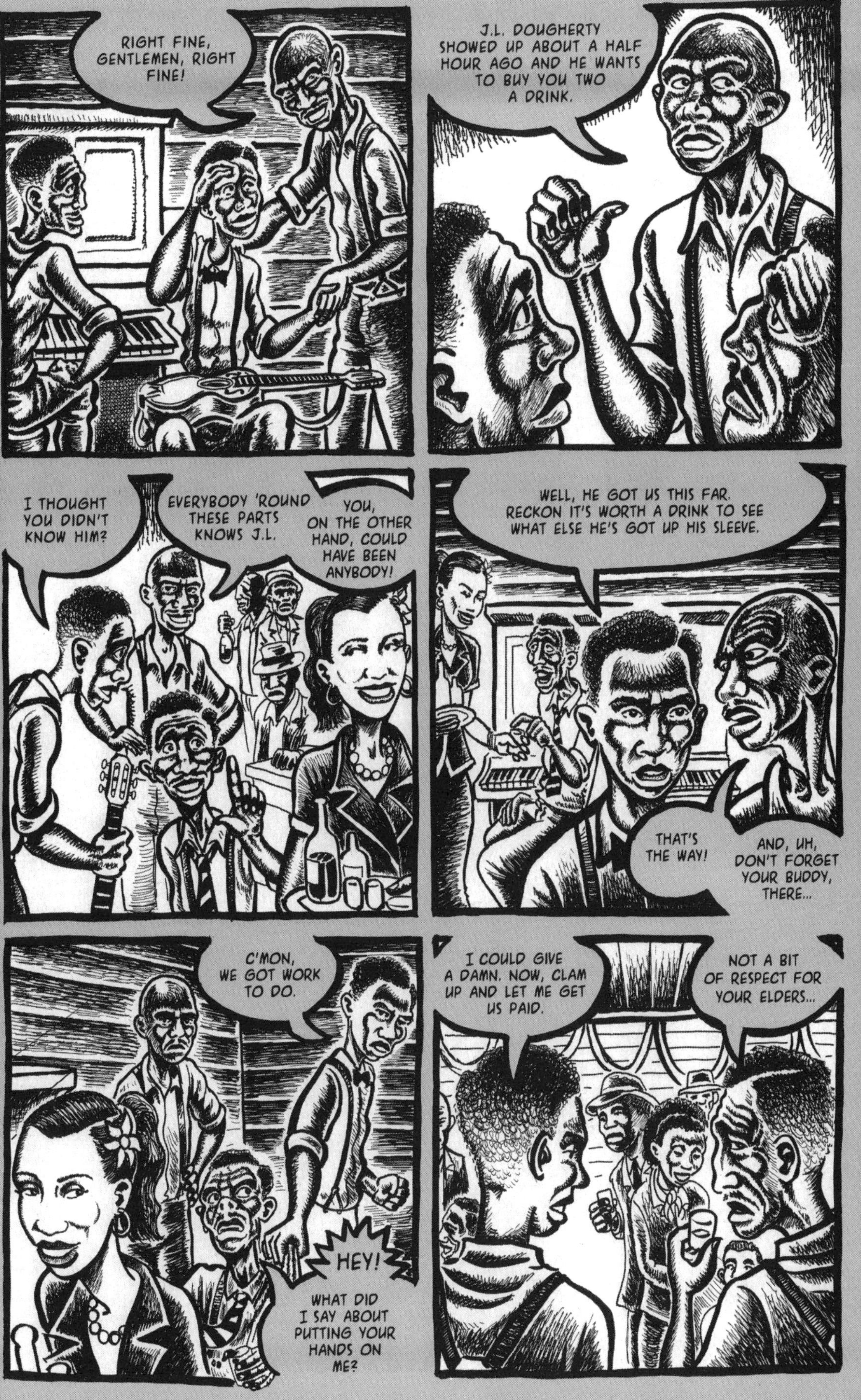
RIGHT FINE, GENTLEMEN, RIGHT FINE!
J.L. DOUGHERTY SHOWED UP ABOUT A HALF HOUR AGO AND HE WANTS TO BUY YOU TWO A DRINK.
I THOUGHT YOU DIDN'T KNOW HIM?
EVERYBODY 'ROUND THESE PARTS KNOWS J.L.
YOU, ON THE OTHER HAND, COULD HAVE BEEN ANYBODY!
WELL, HE GOT US THIS FAR. RECKON IT'S WORTH A DRINK TO SEE WHAT ELSE HE'S GOT UP HIS SLEEVE.
THAT'S THE WAY!
AND, UH, DON'T FORGET YOUR BUDDY, THERE...
C'MON, WE GOT WORK TO DO.
HEY!
WHAT DID I SAY ABOUT PUTTING YOUR HANDS ON ME?
I COULD GIVE A DAMN. NOW, CLAM UP AND LET ME GET US PAID.
NOT A BIT OF RESPECT FOR YOUR ELDERS...

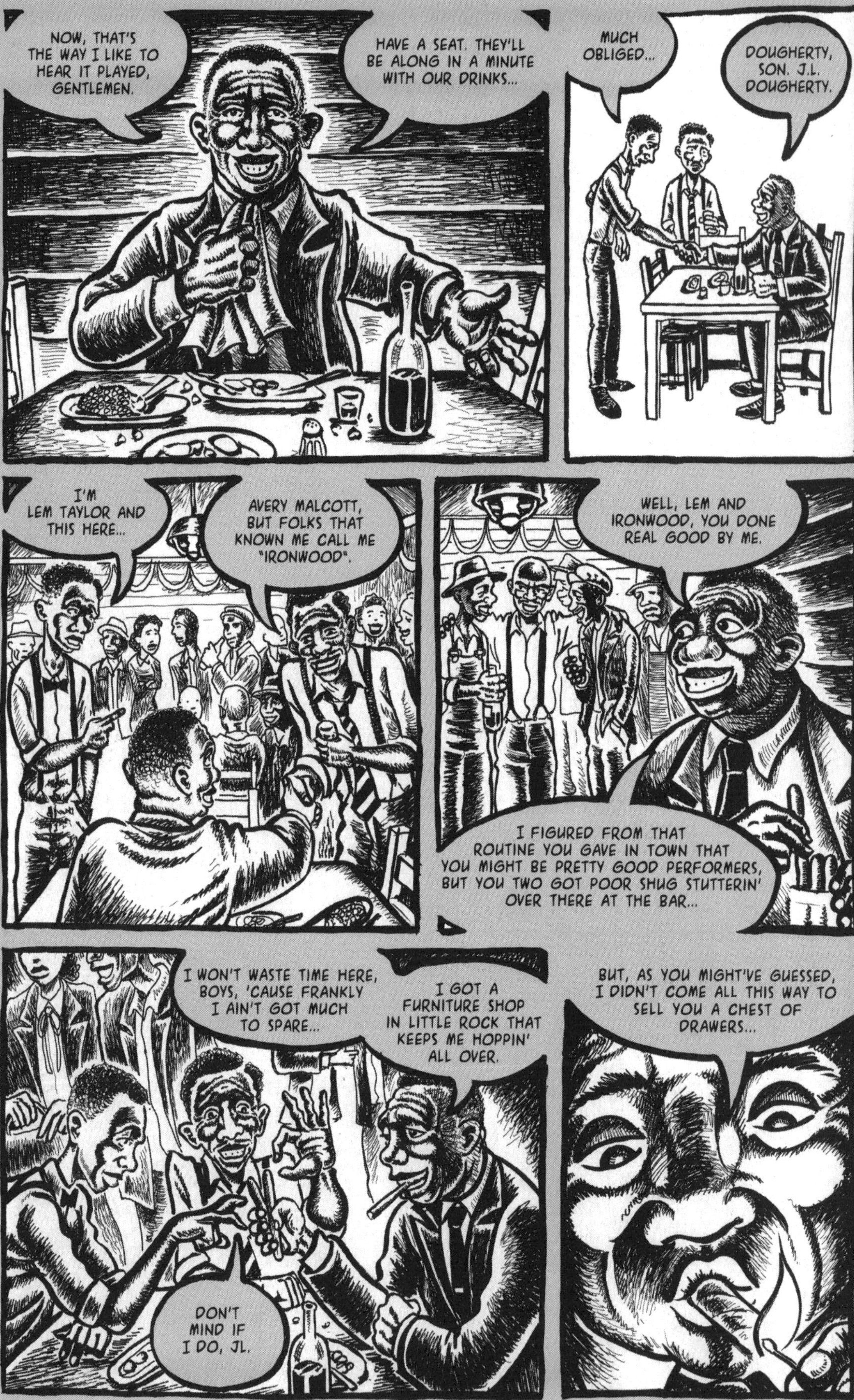
NOW, THAT'S THE WAY I LIKE TO HEAR IT PLAYED, GENTLEMEN.
HAVE A SEAT. THEY'LL BE ALONG IN A MINUTE WITH OUR DRINKS...
MUCH OBLIGED...
DOUGHERTY, SON. J.L. DOUGHERTY.
I'M LEM TAYLOR AND THIS HERE...
AVERY MALCOTT, BUT FOLKS THAT KNOWN ME CALL ME "IRONWOOD".
WELL, LEM AND IRONWOOD, YOU DONE REAL GOOD BY ME.
I FIGURED FROM THAT ROUTINE YOU GAVE IN TOWN THAT YOU MIGHT BE PRETTY GOOD PERFORMERS, BUT YOU TWO GOT POOR SHUG STUTTERIN' OVER THERE AT THE BAR...
I WON'T WASTE TIME HERE, BOYS, 'CAUSE FRANKLY I AIN'T GOT MUCH TO SPARE...
I GOT A FURNITURE SHOP IN LITTLE ROCK THAT KEEPS ME HOPPIN' ALL OVER.
DON'T MIND IF I DO, JL.
BUT, AS YOU MIGHT'VE GUESSED, I DIDN'T COME ALL THIS WAY TO SELL YOU A CHEST OF DRAWERS...

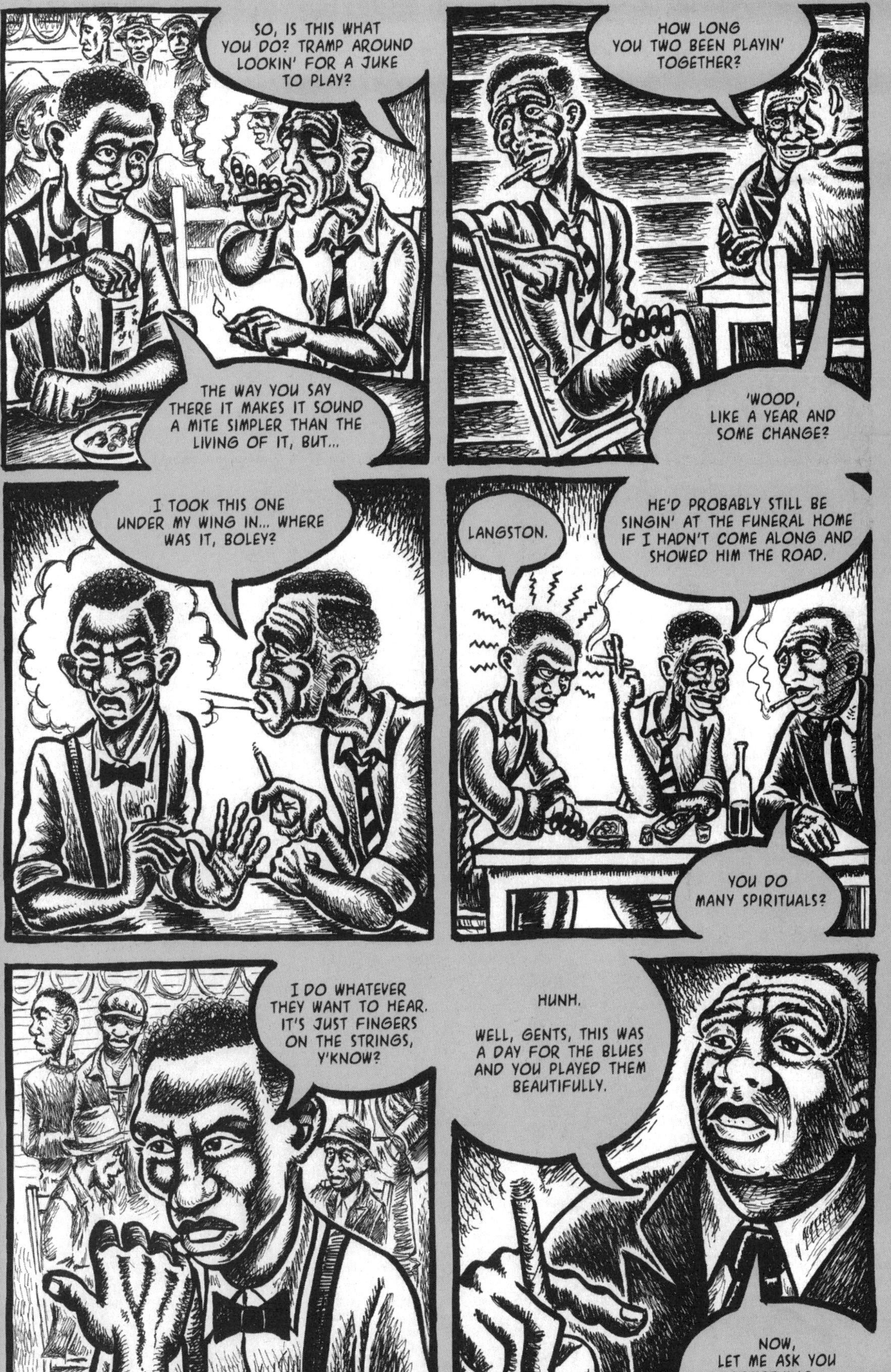
SO, IS THIS WHAT YOU DO? TRAMP AROUND LOOKIN' FOR A JUKE TO PLAY?
THE WAY YOU SAY THERE IT MAKES IT SOUND A MITE SIMPLER THAN THE LIVING OF IT, BUT...
HOW LONG YOU TWO BEEN PLAYIN' TOGETHER?
'WOOD, LIKE A YEAR AND SOME CHANGE?
I TOOK THIS ONE UNDER MY WING IN... WHERE WAS IT, BOLEY?
LANGSTON.
HE'D PROBABLY STILL BE SINGIN' AT THE FUNERAL HOME IF I HADN'T COME ALONG AND SHOWED HIM THE ROAD.
YOU DO MANY SPIRITUALS?
I DO WHATEVER THEY WANT TO HEAR. IT'S JUST FINGERS ON THE STRINGS, Y'KNOW?
HUNH.
WELL, GENTS, THIS WAS A DAY FOR THE BLUES AND YOU PLAYED THEM BEAUTIFULLY.
NOW, LET ME ASK YOU SOMETHING...

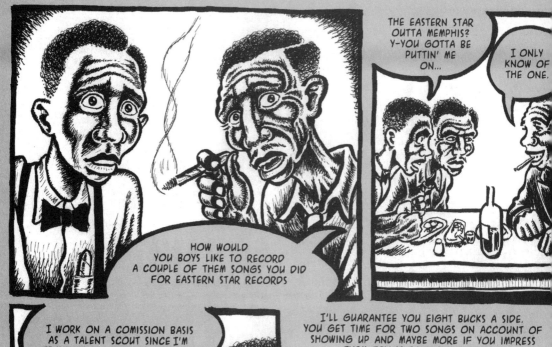

THE EASTERN STAR OUTTA MEMPHIS? Y-YOU GOTTA BE PUTTIN' ME ON...

I ONLY KNOW OF THE ONE.

HOW WOULD YOU BOYS LIKE TO RECORD A COUPLE OF THEM SONGS YOU DID FOR EASTERN STAR RECORDS

I WORK ON A COMISSION BASIS AS A TALENT SCOUT SINCE I'M TRAVELIN' ALL THE TIME ANYWAY.

'WOOD, THAT'S THE SAME PLACE WHERE LEMON GOT HIS START...

I'LL GUARANTEE YOU EIGHT BUCKS A SIDE. YOU GET TIME FOR TWO SONGS ON ACCOUNT OF SHOWING UP AND MAYBE MORE IF YOU IMPRESS THEM FELLAS BEHIND THE BOARD. YOU THINK YOU COULD MAKE MEMPHIS IN A WEEK?

NO POWER IN HEAVEN OR EARTH COULD KEEP US FROM IT, MR. DOUGHERTY. THANK YOU!

IF YOU FELLAS SOUND HALF AS GOOD ON A VICTROLA AS YOU DID HERE TONIGHT, IT'LL BE ME THANKING YOU WHEN WE GET THE SALES FIGURES BACK.

THAT'S FOUR A MAN... FOR ONE TUNE.

SHUG, THAT'S WAS ONE HELL OF A DINNER.

I REALLY APPRECIATE YOUR TAKING THESE TWO IN, SO THERE'S A LITTLE SOMETHING EXTRA FOR YOU HERE.

THANKS AGAIN, JL, FOR STOPPING BY.

ANYTHING YOU NEED, YOU KNOW I AM THE ONE!

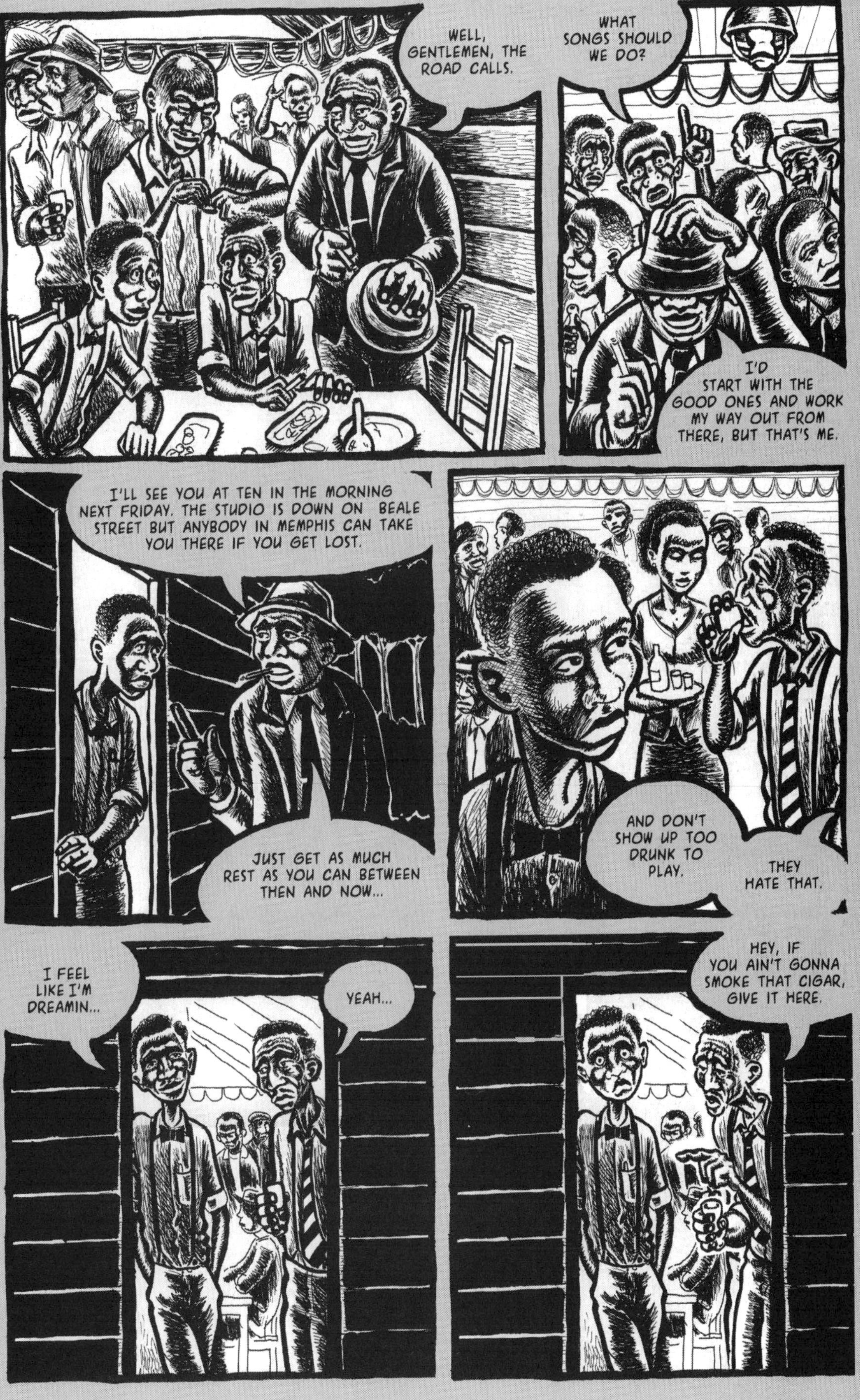
WELL, GENTLEMEN, THE ROAD CALLS.
WHAT SONGS SHOULD WE DO?
I'D START WITH THE GOOD ONES AND WORK MY WAY OUT FROM THERE, BUT THAT'S ME.
I'LL SEE YOU AT TEN IN THE MORNING NEXT FRIDAY. THE STUDIO IS DOWN ON BEALE STREET BUT ANYBODY IN MEMPHIS CAN TAKE YOU THERE IF YOU GET LOST.
JUST GET AS MUCH REST AS YOU CAN BETWEEN THEN AND NOW...
AND DON'T SHOW UP TOO DRUNK TO PLAY.
THEY HATE THAT.
I FEEL LIKE I'M DREAMIN...
YEAH...
HEY, IF YOU AIN'T GONNA SMOKE THAT CIGAR, GIVE IT HERE.

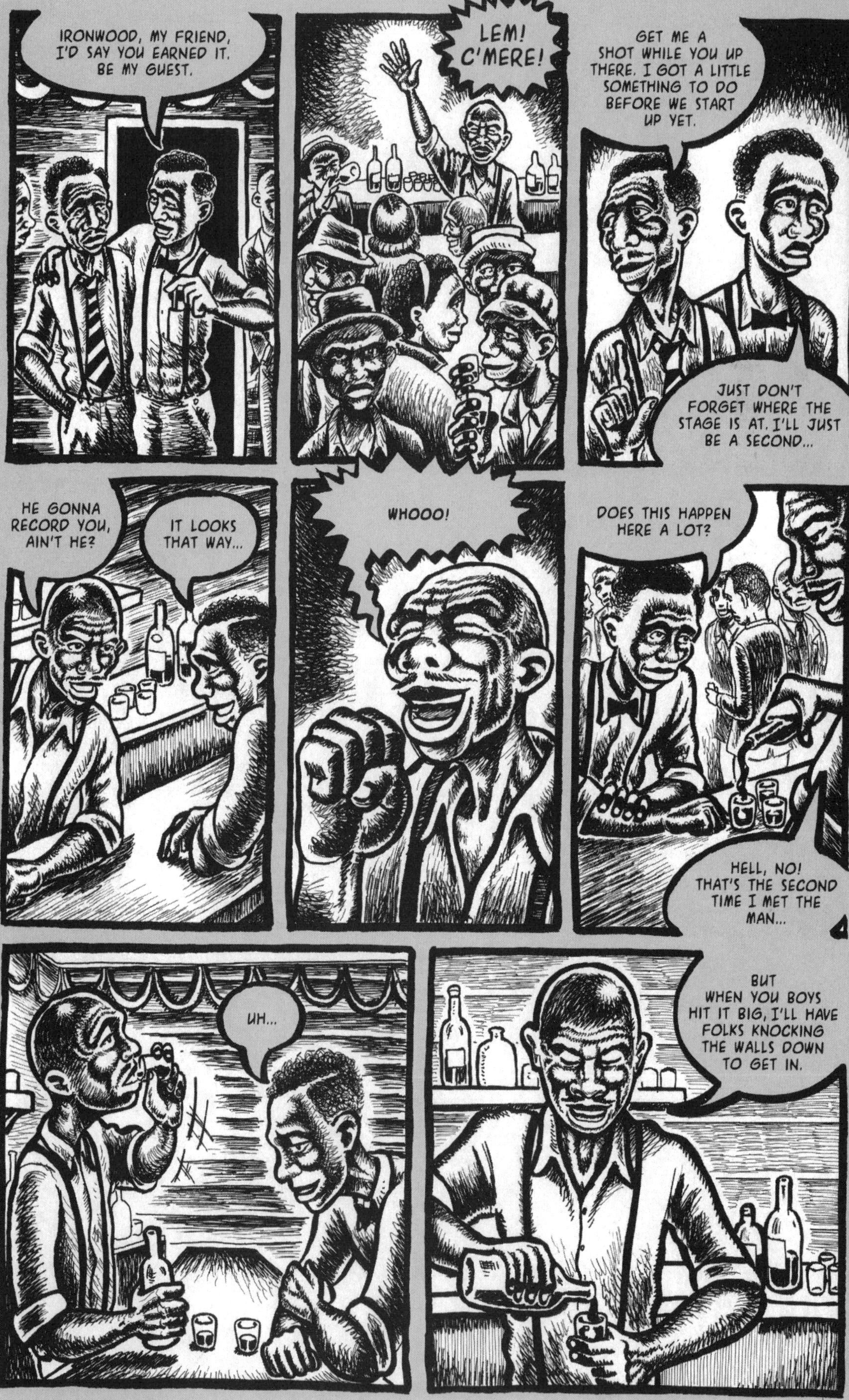

IRONWOOD, MY FRIEND, I'D SAY YOU EARNED IT. BE MY GUEST.
LEM! C'MERE!
GET ME A SHOT WHILE YOU UP THERE. I GOT A LITTLE SOMETHING TO DO BEFORE WE START UP YET.
JUST DON'T FORGET WHERE THE STAGE IS AT. I'LL JUST BE A SECOND...
HE GONNA RECORD YOU, AIN'T HE?
IT LOOKS THAT WAY...
WHOOO!
DOES THIS HAPPEN HERE A LOT?
HELL, NO! THAT'S THE SECOND TIME I MET THE MAN...
UH...
BUT WHEN YOU BOYS HIT IT BIG, I'LL HAVE FOLKS KNOCKING THE WALLS DOWN TO GET IN.

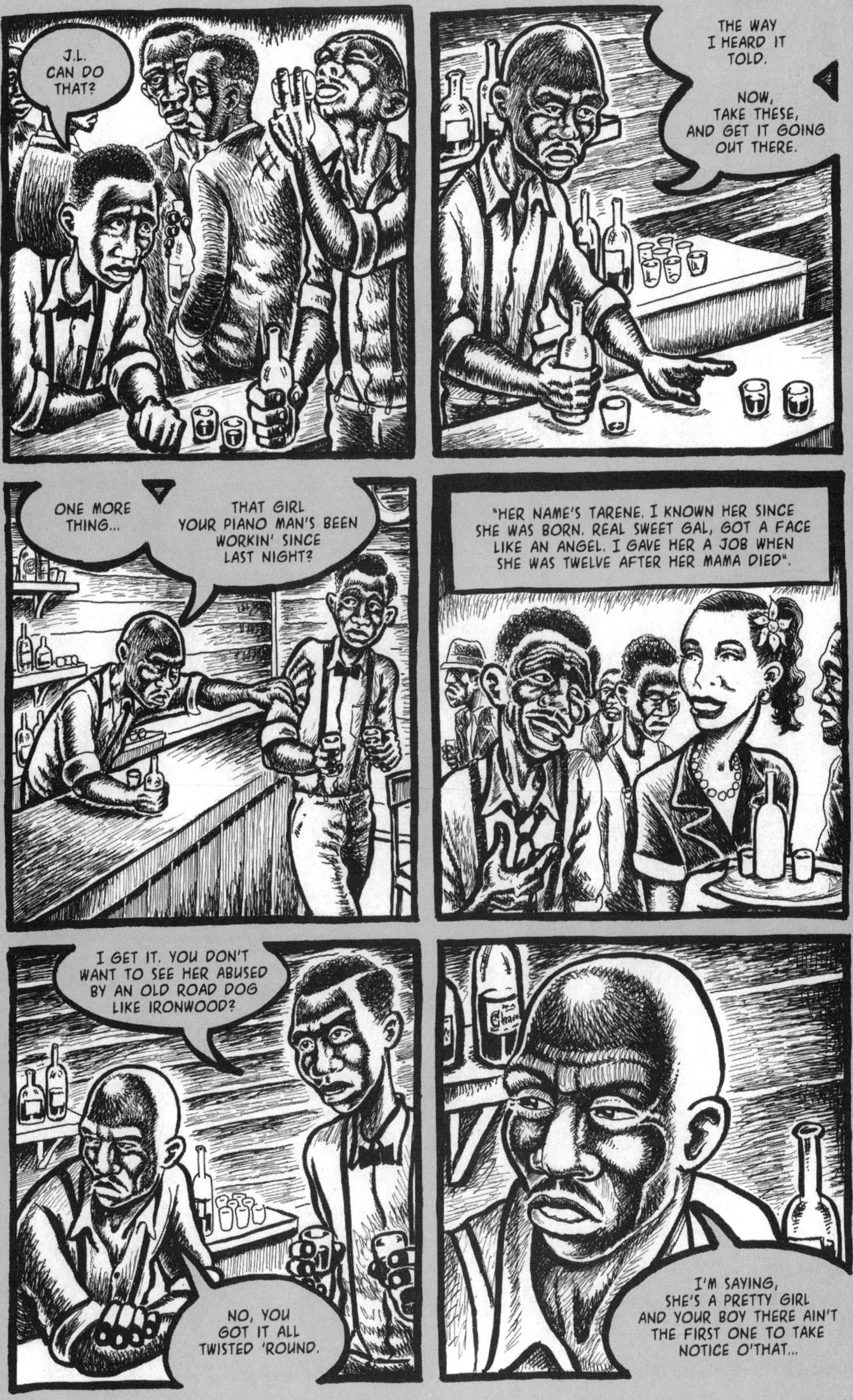
J.L. CAN DO THAT?
THE WAY I HEARD IT TOLD.
NOW, TAKE THESE, AND GET IT GOING OUT THERE.
ONE MORE THING...
THAT GIRL YOUR PIANO MAN'S BEEN WORKIN' SINCE LAST NIGHT?
"HER NAME'S TARENE. I KNOWN HER SINCE SHE WAS BORN. REAL SWEET GAL, GOT A FACE LIKE AN ANGEL. I GAVE HER A JOB WHEN SHE WAS TWELVE AFTER HER MAMA DIED".
I GET IT. YOU DON'T WANT TO SEE HER ABUSED BY AN OLD ROAD DOG LIKE IRONWOOD?
NO, YOU GOT IT ALL TWISTED 'ROUND.
I'M SAYING, SHE'S A PRETTY GIRL AND YOUR BOY THERE AIN'T THE FIRST ONE TO TAKE NOTICE O'THAT...

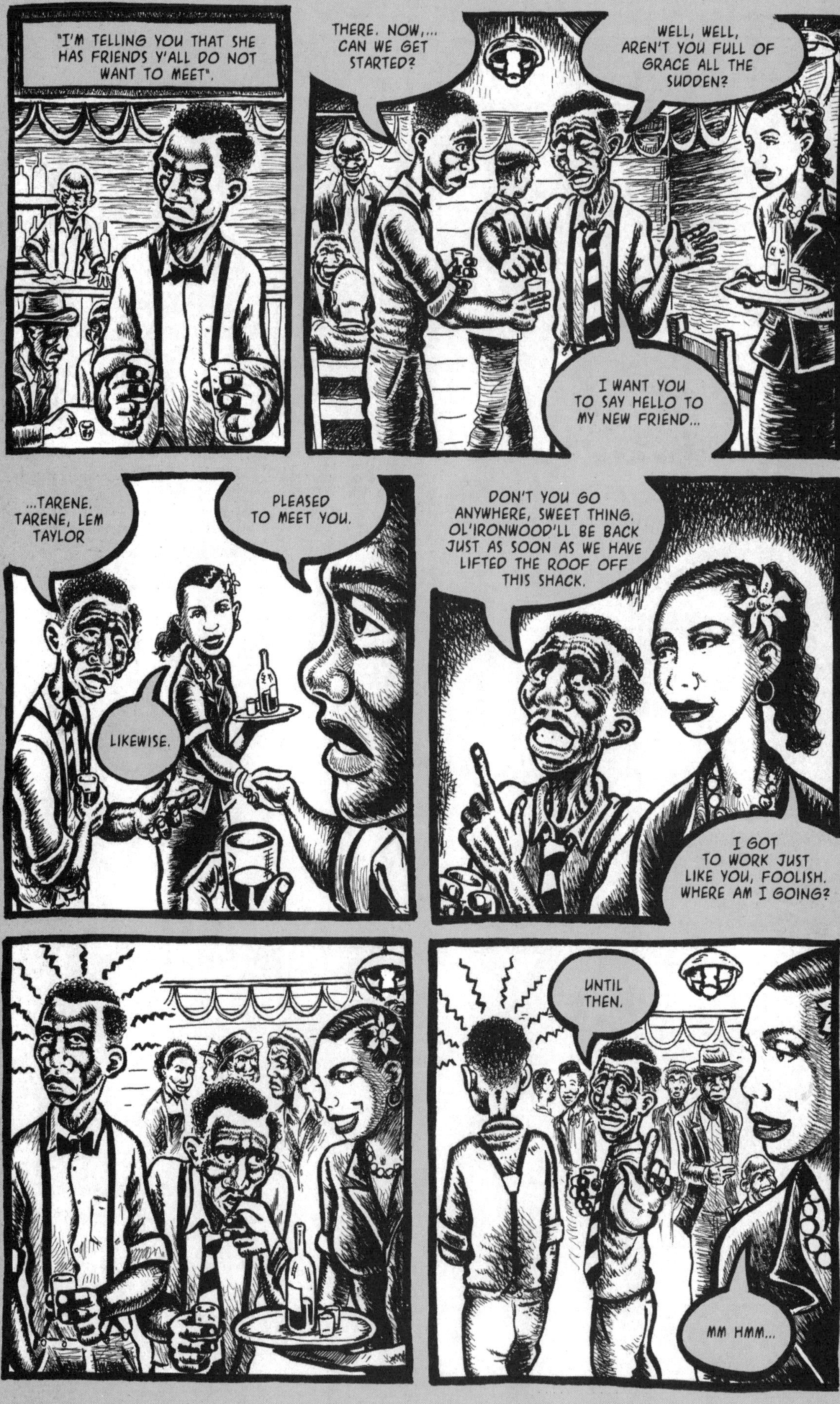
"I'M TELLING YOU THAT SHE HAS FRIENDS Y'ALL DO NOT WANT TO MEET".
THERE. NOW,... CAN WE GET STARTED?
WELL, WELL, AREN'T YOU FULL OF GRACE ALL THE SUDDEN?
I WANT YOU TO SAY HELLO TO MY NEW FRIEND...
...TARENE. TARENE, LEM TAYLOR
PLEASED TO MEET YOU.
LIKEWISE.
DON'T YOU GO ANYWHERE, SWEET THING. OL'IRONWOOD'LL BE BACK JUST AS SOON AS WE HAVE LIFTED THE ROOF OFF THIS SHACK.
I GOT TO WORK JUST LIKE YOU, FOOLISH. WHERE AM I GOING?
UNTIL THEN.
MM HMM...

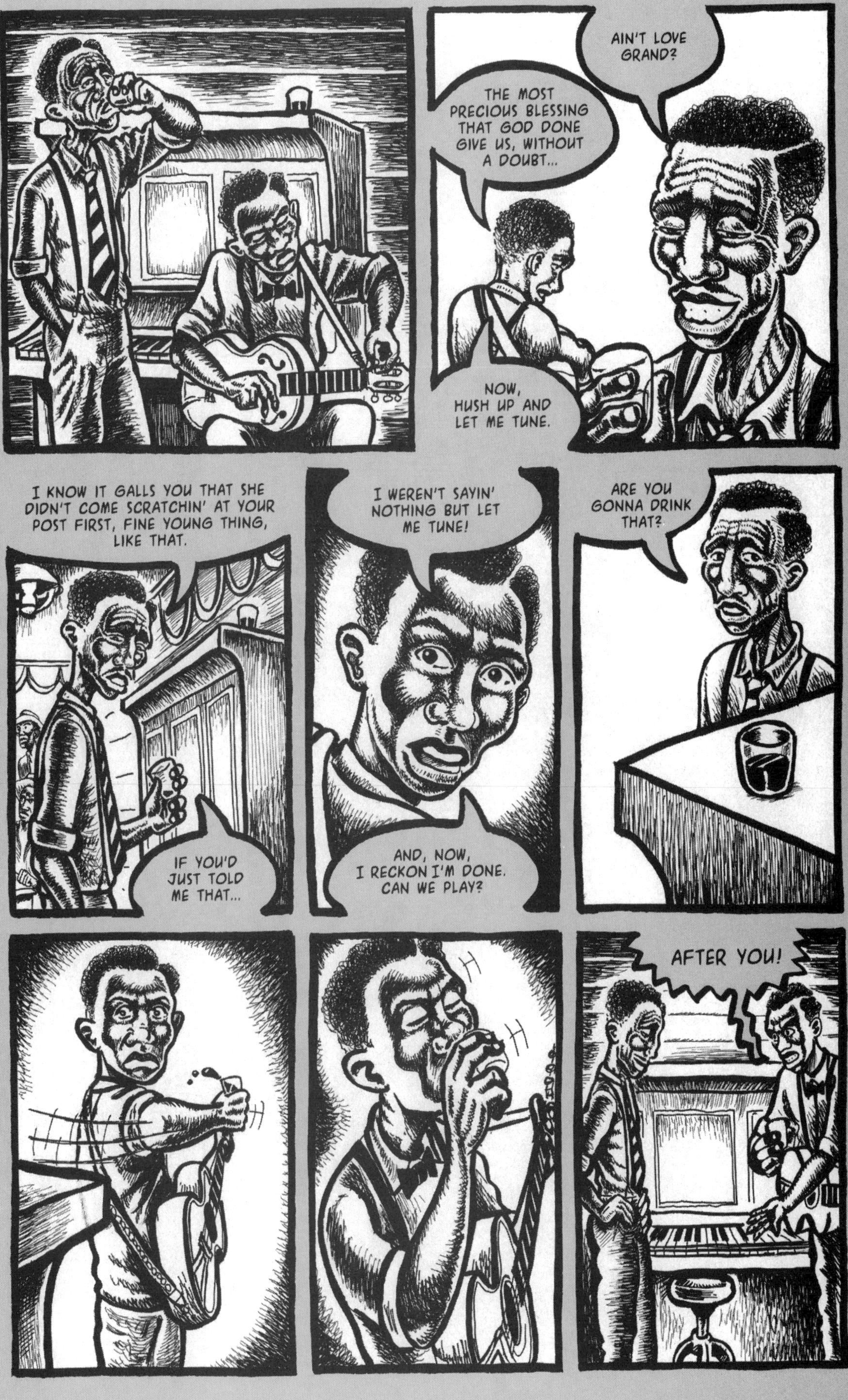
AIN'T LOVE GRAND?
THE MOST PRECIOUS BLESSING THAT GOD DONE GIVE US, WITHOUT A DOUBT...
NOW, HUSH UP AND LET ME TUNE.
I KNOW IT GALLS YOU THAT SHE DIDN'T COME SCRATCHIN' AT YOUR POST FIRST, FINE YOUNG THING, LIKE THAT.
IF YOU'D JUST TOLD ME THAT...
I WEREN'T SAYIN' NOTHING BUT LET ME TUNE!
AND, NOW, I RECKON I'M DONE. CAN WE PLAY?
ARE YOU GONNA DRINK THAT?
AFTER YOU!

"These periods of relative comfort, momentarily plugged into a community of support normally denied to them by virtue of their very function..."

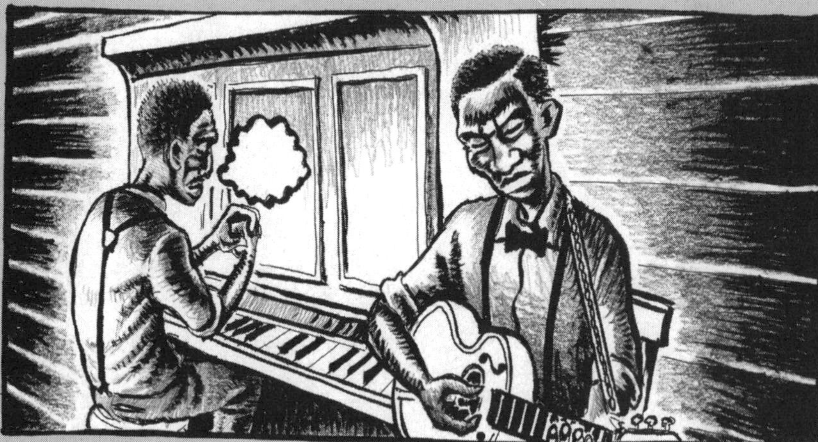

"... were the moments that kept these musicians walking the roads, putting one foot in front of the other..."

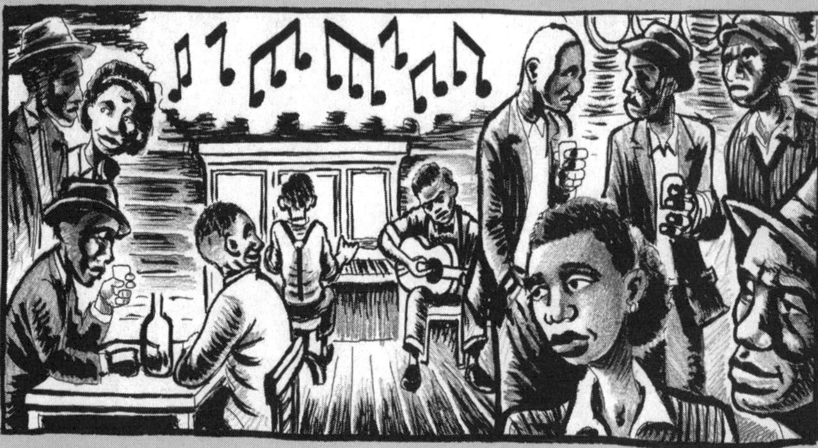

"... to find the next juke that would pay off even bigger than the last one.

For as sure as it seemed that there was some kind of hope, just up around the bend..."

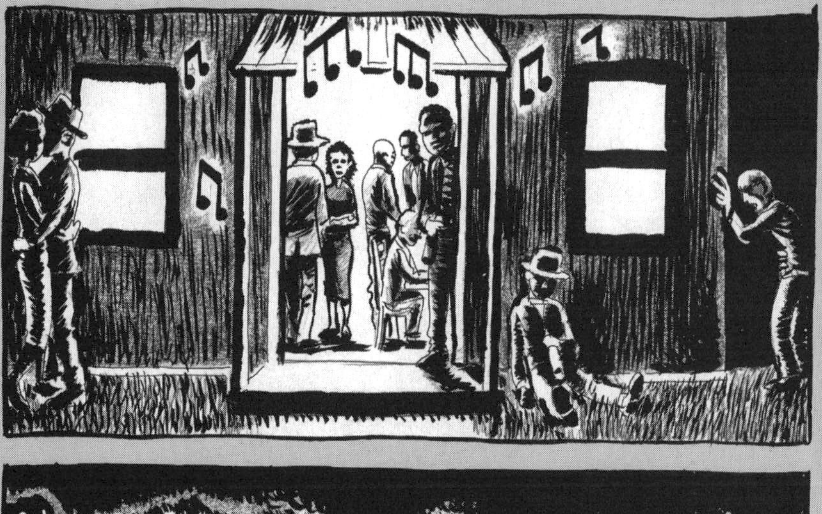

... "it was no secret that catastrophe was just as likely to take them before they arrived"...

"The Roots of British R&B: Blind Lemon Jefferson to T-Bone Walker"
Ira Deldoff
(New Sounds, pg. 14, Issue 7, 1966)

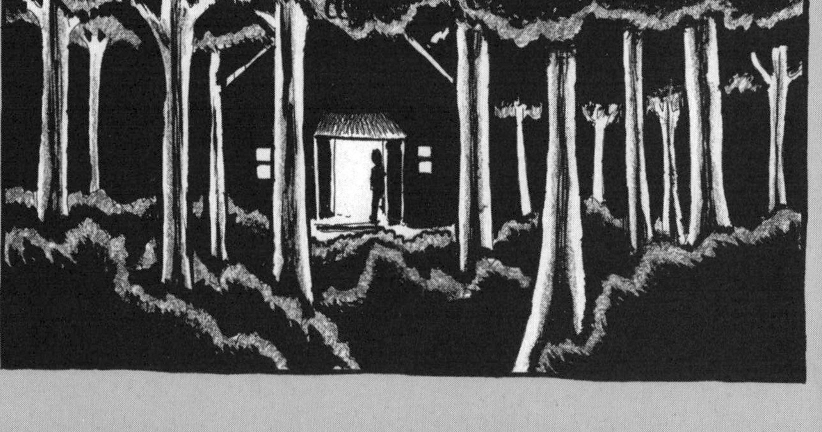

4

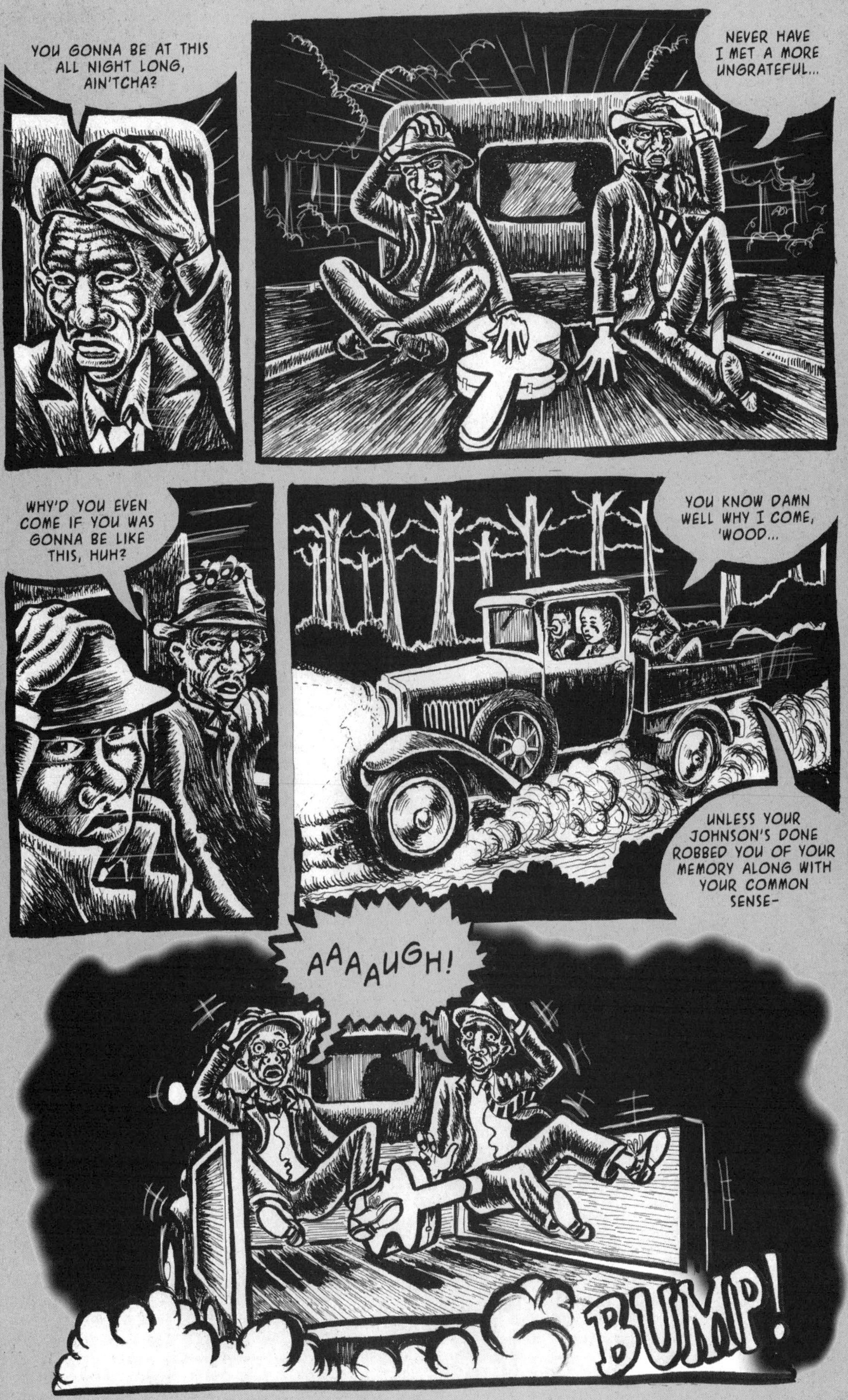
YOU GONNA BE AT THIS ALL NIGHT LONG, AIN'TCHA?
NEVER HAVE I MET A MORE UNGRATEFUL...
WHY'D YOU EVEN COME IF YOU WAS GONNA BE LIKE THIS, HUH?
YOU KNOW DAMN WELL WHY I COME, 'WOOD...
UNLESS YOUR JOHNSON'S DONE ROBBED YOU OF YOUR MEMORY ALONG WITH YOUR COMMON SENSE-
AAAAUGH!
BUMP!

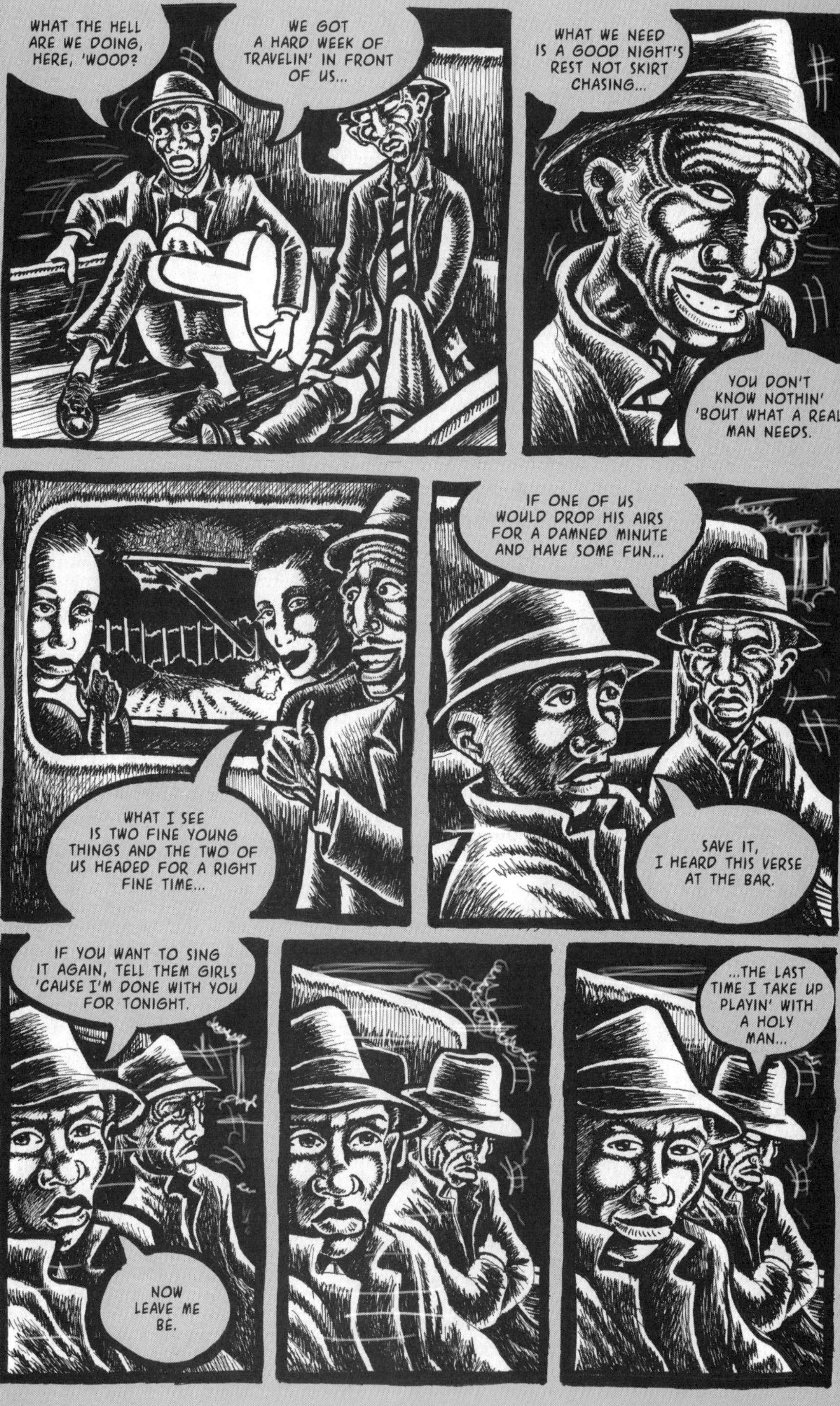
WHAT THE HELL ARE WE DOING, HERE, 'WOOD?
WE GOT A HARD WEEK OF TRAVELIN' IN FRONT OF US...
WHAT WE NEED IS A GOOD NIGHT'S REST NOT SKIRT CHASING...
YOU DON'T KNOW NOTHIN' 'BOUT WHAT A REAL MAN NEEDS.
WHAT I SEE IS TWO FINE YOUNG THINGS AND THE TWO OF US HEADED FOR A RIGHT FINE TIME...
IF ONE OF US WOULD DROP HIS AIRS FOR A DAMNED MINUTE AND HAVE SOME FUN...
SAVE IT, I HEARD THIS VERSE AT THE BAR.
IF YOU WANT TO SING IT AGAIN, TELL THEM GIRLS 'CAUSE I'M DONE WITH YOU FOR TONIGHT.
NOW LEAVE ME BE.
...THE LAST TIME I TAKE UP PLAYIN' WITH A HOLY MAN...

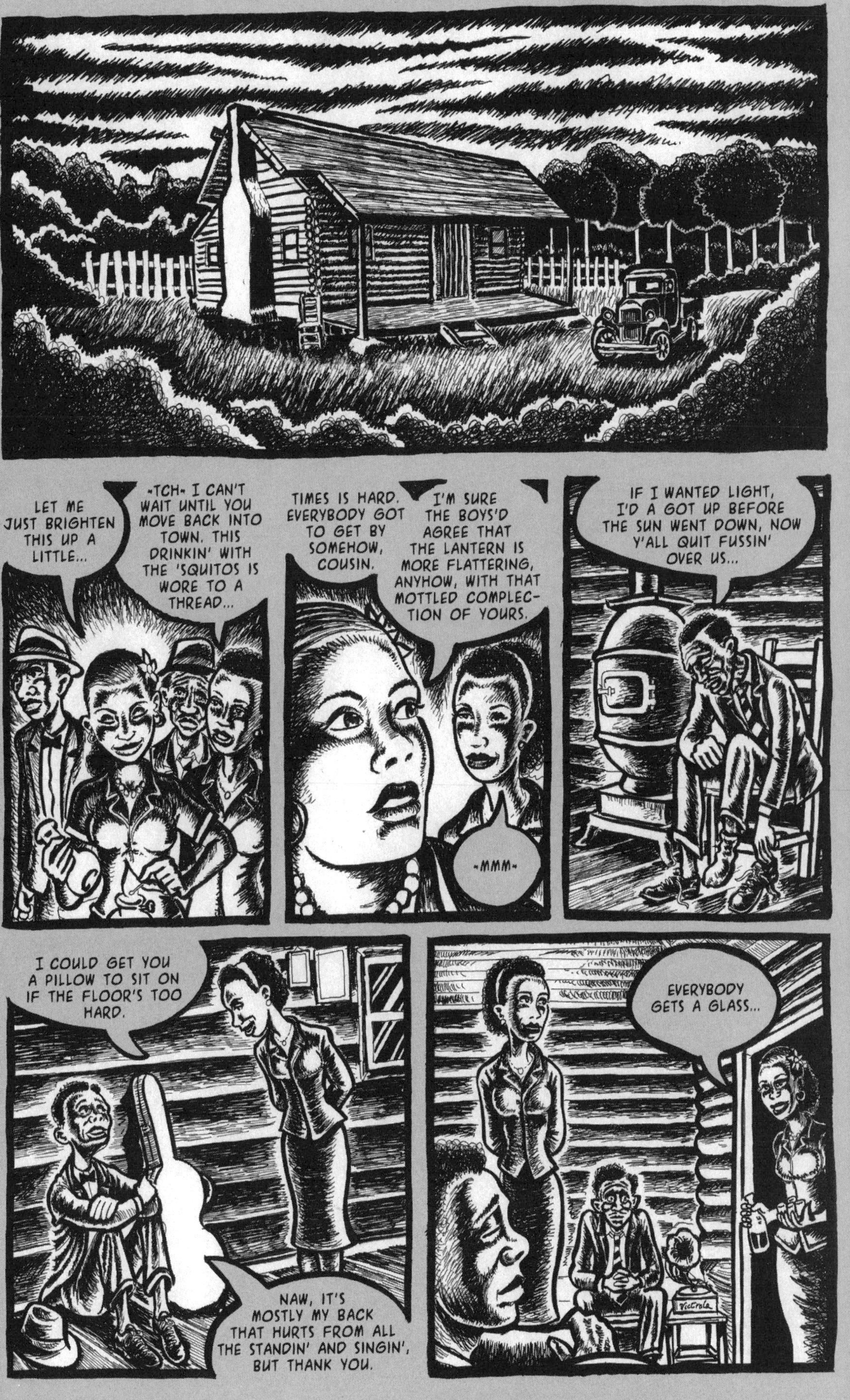
LET ME JUST BRIGHTEN THIS UP A LITTLE...
•TCH• I CAN'T WAIT UNTIL YOU MOVE BACK INTO TOWN. THIS DRINKIN' WITH THE 'SQUITOS IS WORE TO A THREAD...
TIMES IS HARD. EVERYBODY GOT TO GET BY SOMEHOW, COUSIN.
I'M SURE THE BOYS'D AGREE THAT THE LANTERN IS MORE FLATTERING, ANYHOW, WITH THAT MOTTLED COMPLECTION OF YOURS.
•MMM•
IF I WANTED LIGHT, I'D A GOT UP BEFORE THE SUN WENT DOWN, NOW Y'ALL QUIT FUSSIN' OVER US...
I COULD GET YOU A PILLOW TO SIT ON IF THE FLOOR'S TOO HARD.
NAW, IT'S MOSTLY MY BACK THAT HURTS FROM ALL THE STANDIN' AND SINGIN', BUT THANK YOU.
EVERYBODY GETS A GLASS...
Victrola

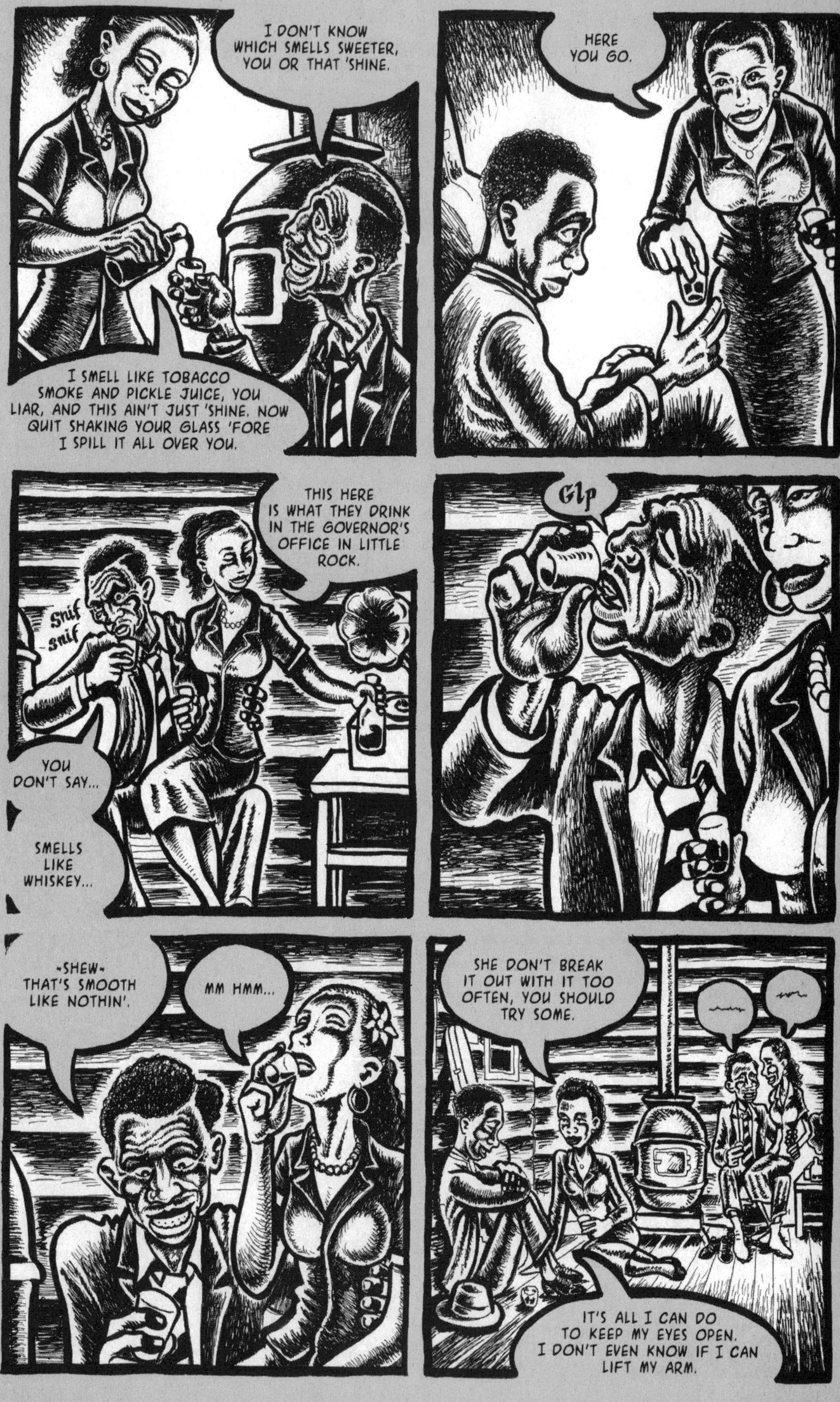
I DON'T KNOW WHICH SMELLS SWEETER, YOU OR THAT 'SHINE.
I SMELL LIKE TOBACCO SMOKE AND PICKLE JUICE, YOU LIAR, AND THIS AIN'T JUST 'SHINE. NOW QUIT SHAKING YOUR GLASS 'FORE I SPILL IT ALL OVER YOU.
HERE YOU GO.
THIS HERE IS WHAT THEY DRINK IN THE GOVERNOR'S OFFICE IN LITTLE ROCK.
Snif snif
YOU DON'T SAY...
SMELLS LIKE WHISKEY...
Glp
~SHEW~ THAT'S SMOOTH LIKE NOTHIN'.
MM HMM...
SHE DON'T BREAK IT OUT WITH IT TOO OFTEN, YOU SHOULD TRY SOME.
IT'S ALL I CAN DO TO KEEP MY EYES OPEN. I DON'T EVEN KNOW IF I CAN LIFT MY ARM.

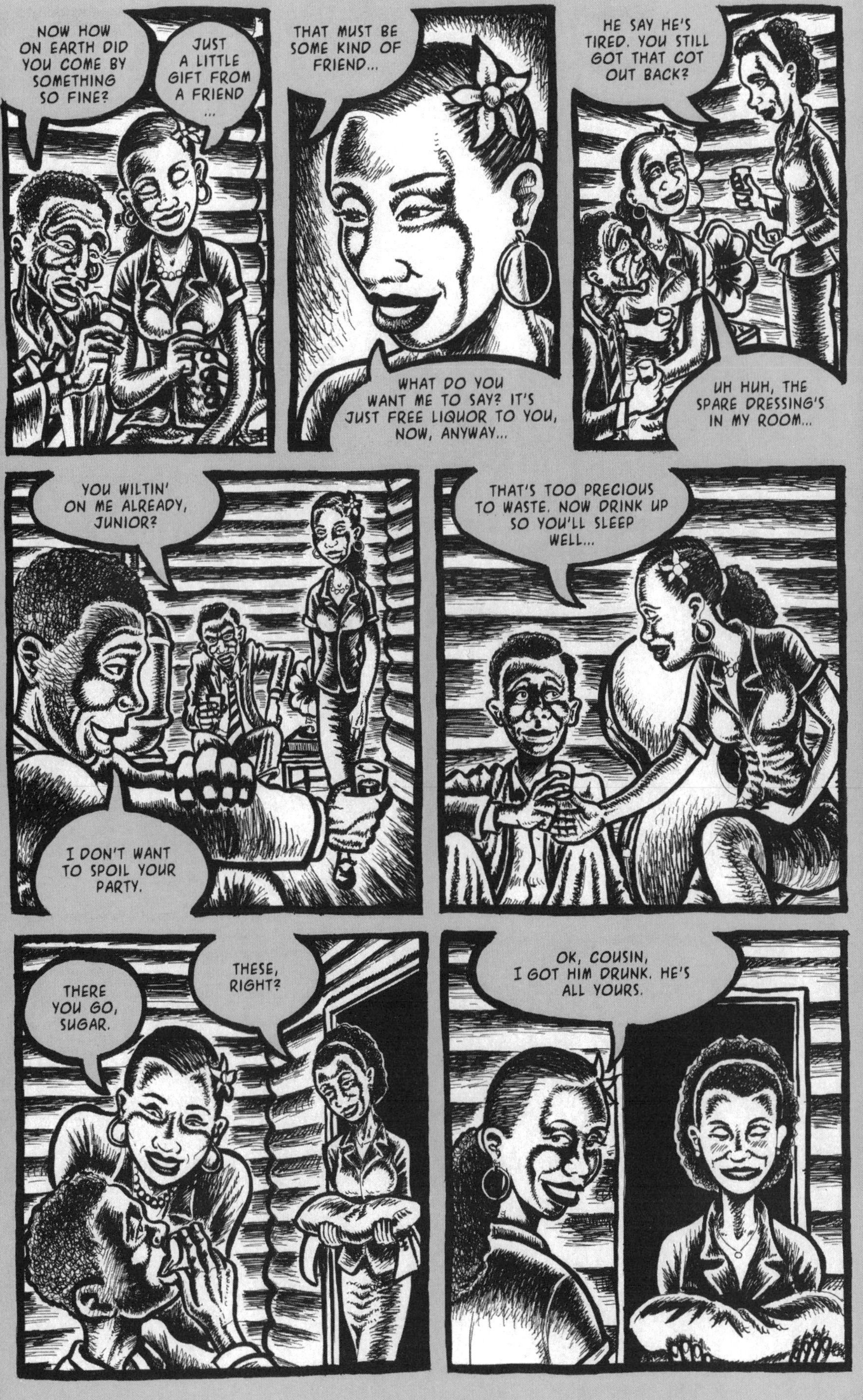
NOW HOW ON EARTH DID YOU COME BY SOMETHING SO FINE?
JUST A LITTLE GIFT FROM A FRIEND ...
THAT MUST BE SOME KIND OF FRIEND...
WHAT DO YOU WANT ME TO SAY? IT'S JUST FREE LIQUOR TO YOU, NOW, ANYWAY...
HE SAY HE'S TIRED. YOU STILL GOT THAT COT OUT BACK?
UH HUH, THE SPARE DRESSING'S IN MY ROOM...
YOU WILTIN' ON ME ALREADY, JUNIOR?
I DON'T WANT TO SPOIL YOUR PARTY.
THAT'S TOO PRECIOUS TO WASTE. NOW DRINK UP SO YOU'LL SLEEP WELL...
THERE YOU GO, SUGAR.
THESE, RIGHT?
OK, COUSIN, I GOT HIM DRUNK. HE'S ALL YOURS.

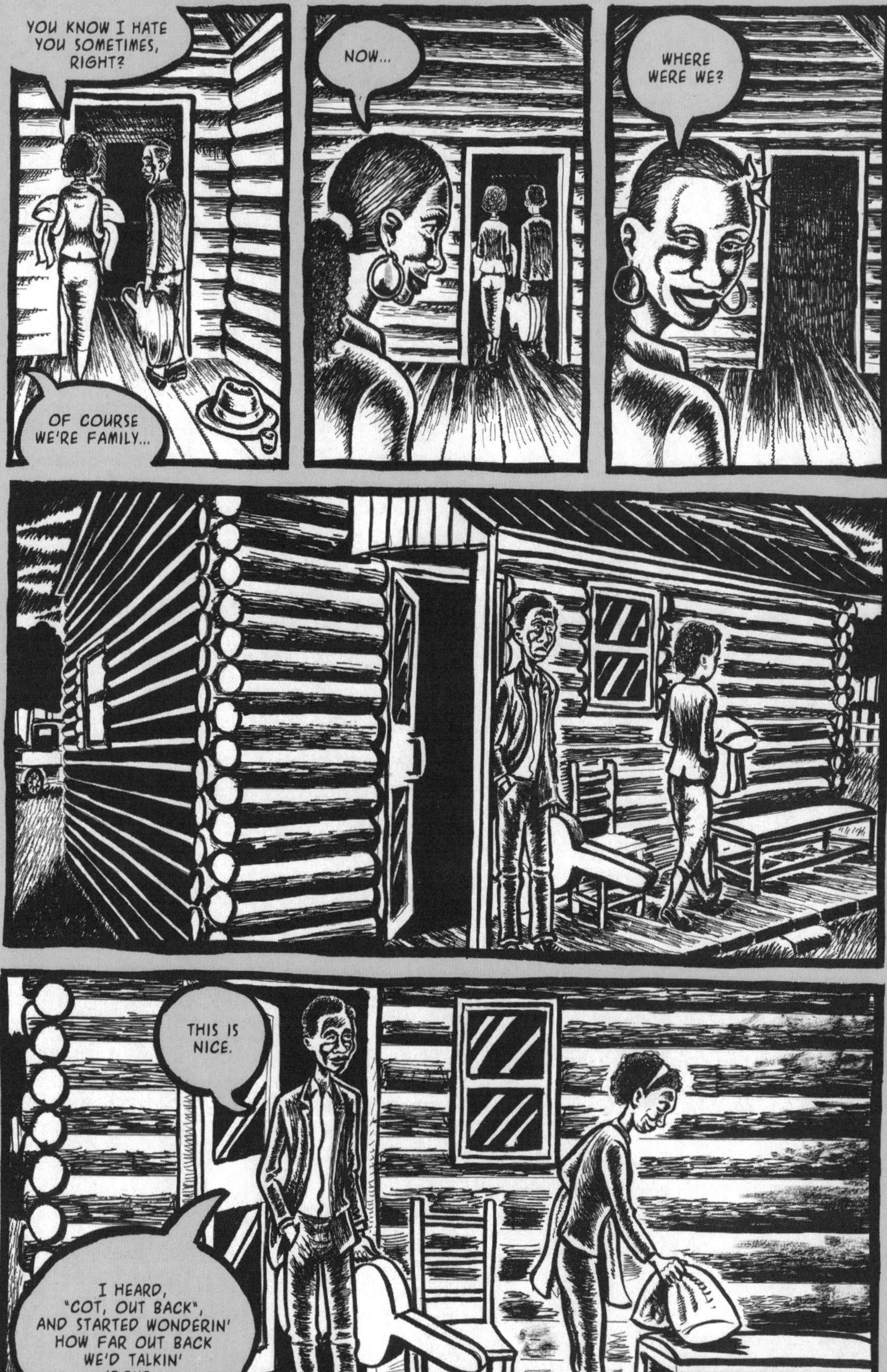
YOU KNOW I HATE YOU SOMETIMES, RIGHT?
OF COURSE WE'RE FAMILY...
NOW...
WHERE WERE WE?
THIS IS NICE.
I HEARD, "COT, OUT BACK", AND STARTED WONDERIN' HOW FAR OUT BACK WE'D TALKIN' 'BOUT...

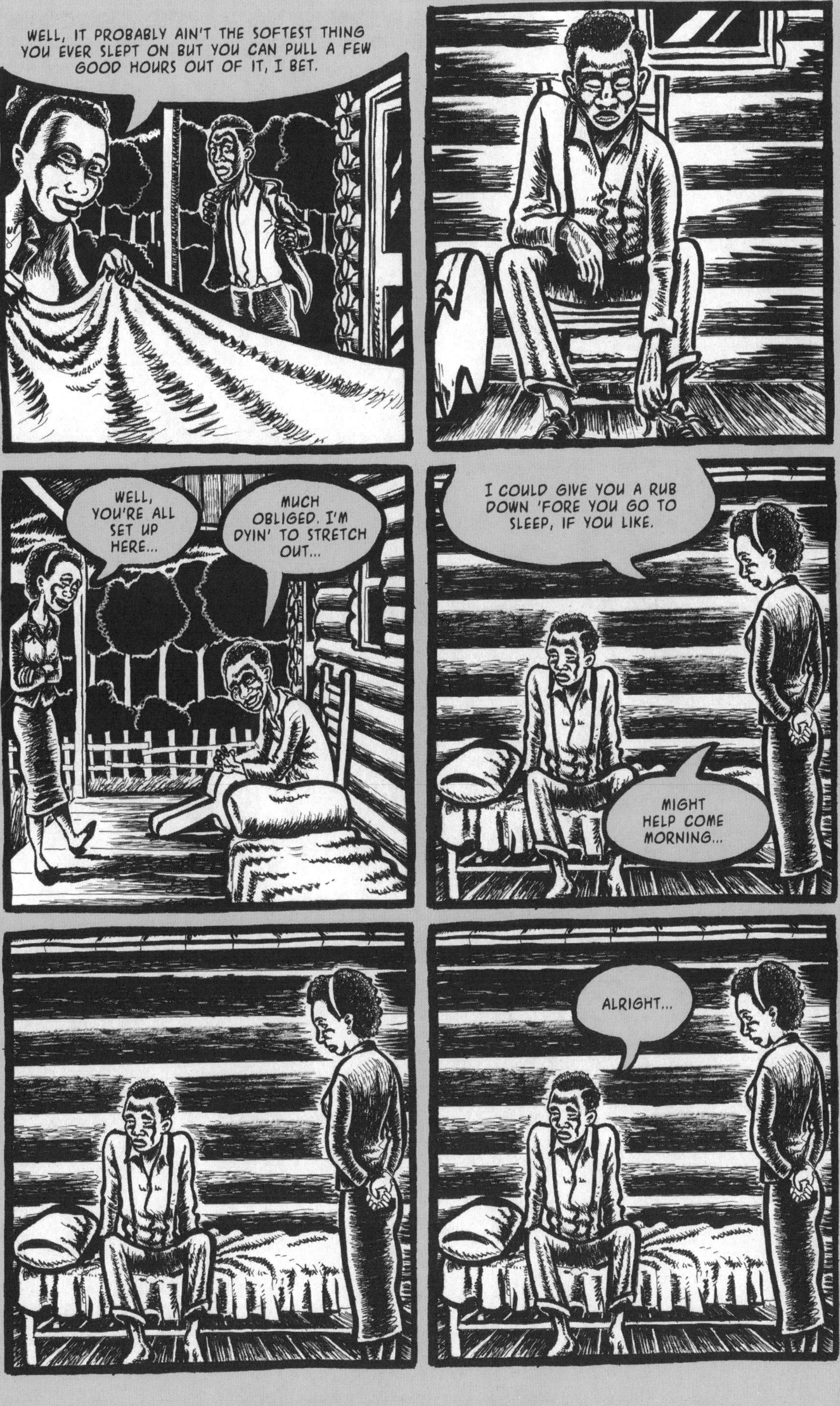
WELL, IT PROBABLY AIN'T THE SOFTEST THING YOU EVER SLEPT ON BUT YOU CAN PULL A FEW GOOD HOURS OUT OF IT, I BET.
WELL, YOU'RE ALL SET UP HERE...
MUCH OBLIGED. I'M DYIN' TO STRETCH OUT...
I COULD GIVE YOU A RUB DOWN 'FORE YOU GO TO SLEEP, IF YOU LIKE.
MIGHT HELP COME MORNING...
ALRIGHT...

GIVE ME YOUR SHIRT AND LAY ON YOUR BELLY.
~ UNNH ~
YOU'RE TIGHT AS BAILIN' WIRE.
WHEN'S THE LAST TIME YOU SLEPT IN A BED?
~MMH~
LAST NIGHT, BUT IT WASN'T NOTHIN' BUT BOXCARS AND BARNS FOR A MONTH OF SUNDAYS BEFORE THAT...
IT ADD UP IN A WAY THAT ONE NIGHT DON'T FIX...

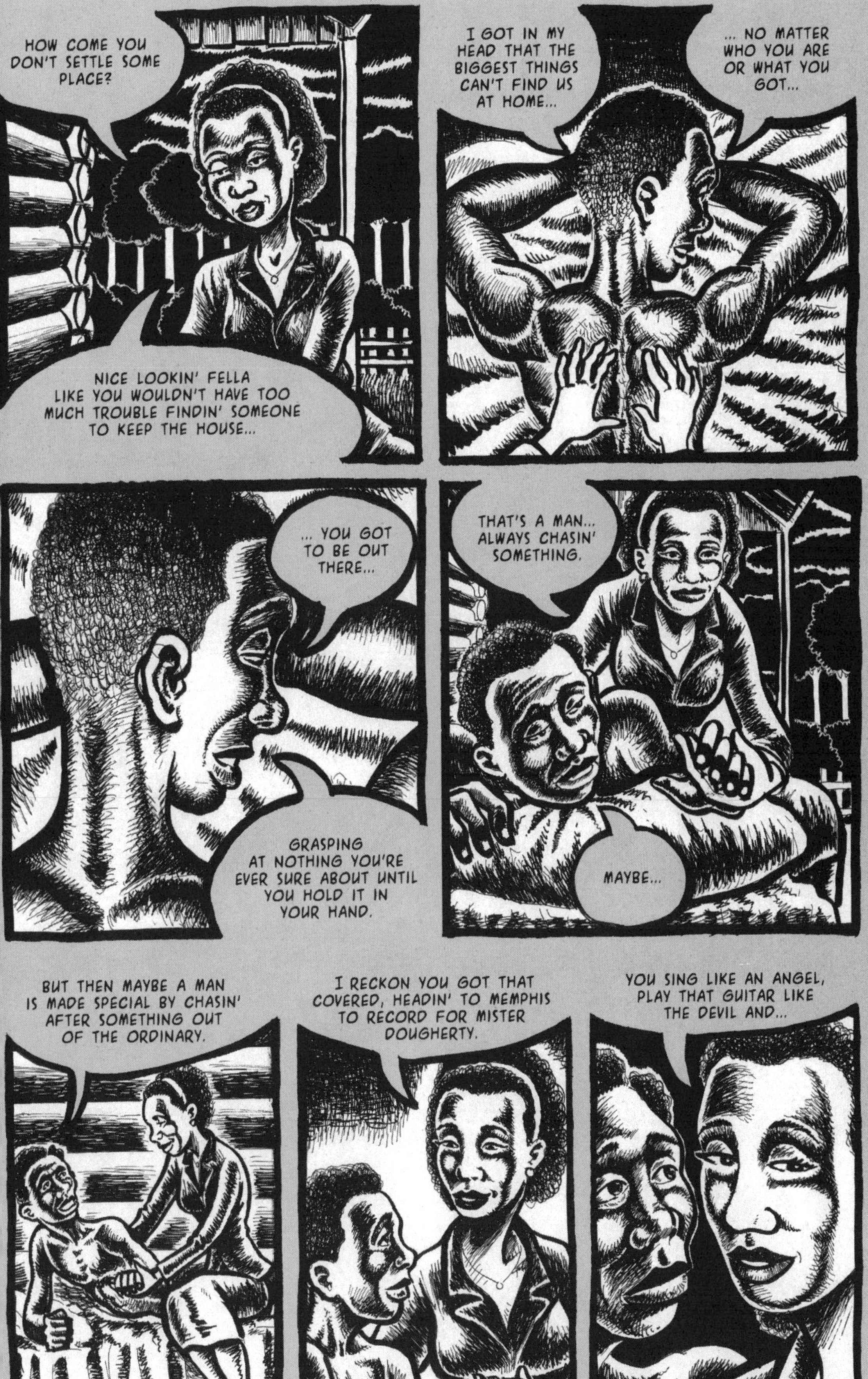
HOW COME YOU DON'T SETTLE SOME PLACE?
NICE LOOKIN' FELLA LIKE YOU WOULDN'T HAVE TOO MUCH TROUBLE FINDIN' SOMEONE TO KEEP THE HOUSE...
I GOT IN MY HEAD THAT THE BIGGEST THINGS CAN'T FIND US AT HOME...
... NO MATTER WHO YOU ARE OR WHAT YOU GOT...
... YOU GOT TO BE OUT THERE...
GRASPING AT NOTHING YOU'RE EVER SURE ABOUT UNTIL YOU HOLD IT IN YOUR HAND.
THAT'S A MAN... ALWAYS CHASIN' SOMETHING.
MAYBE...
BUT THEN MAYBE A MAN IS MADE SPECIAL BY CHASIN' AFTER SOMETHING OUT OF THE ORDINARY.
I RECKON YOU GOT THAT COVERED, HEADIN' TO MEMPHIS TO RECORD FOR MISTER DOUGHERTY.
YOU SING LIKE AN ANGEL, PLAY THAT GUITAR LIKE THE DEVIL AND...

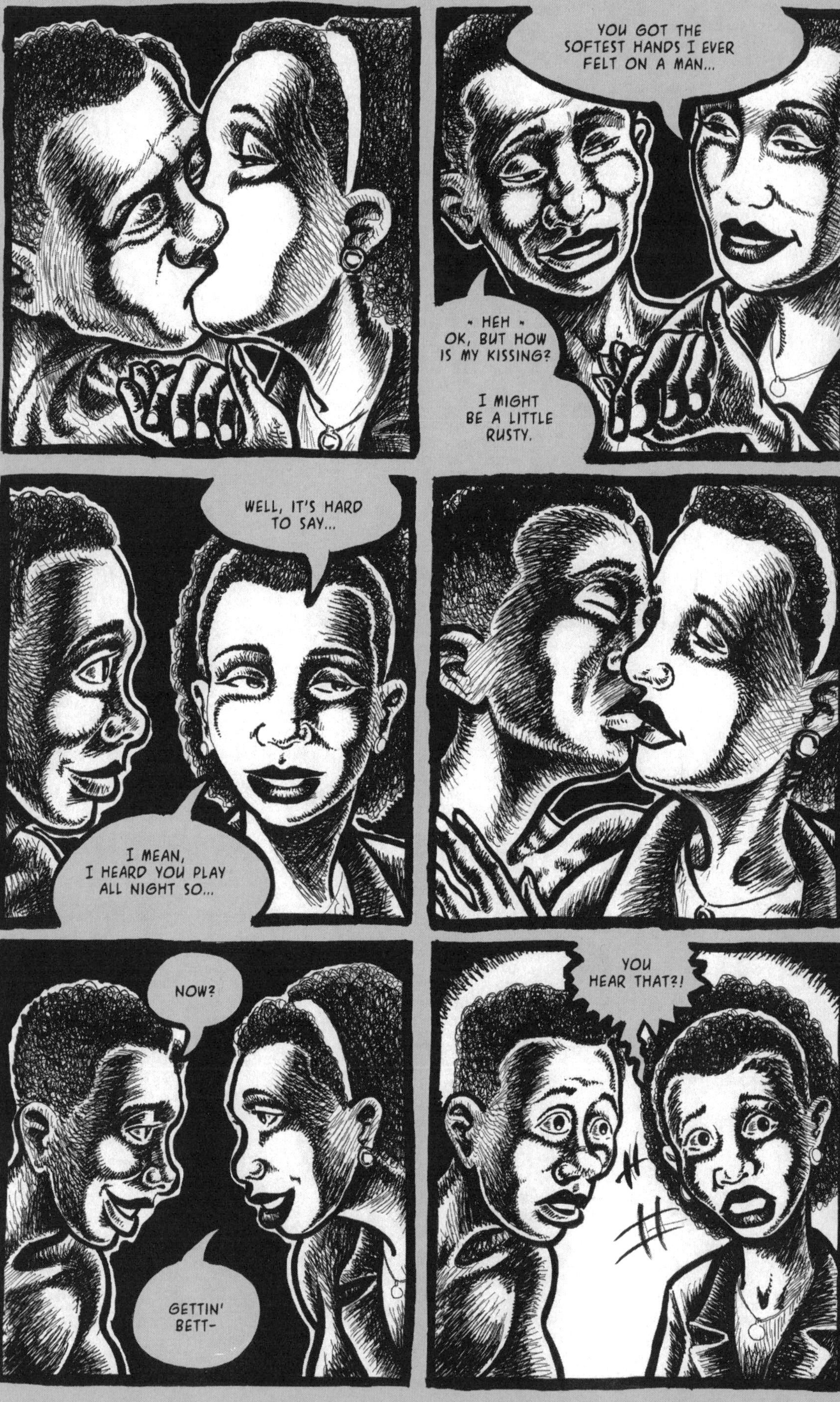
YOU GOT THE SOFTEST HANDS I EVER FELT ON A MAN...
* HEH * OK, BUT HOW IS MY KISSING?
I MIGHT BE A LITTLE RUSTY.
WELL, IT'S HARD TO SAY...
I MEAN, I HEARD YOU PLAY ALL NIGHT SO...
NOW?
GETTIN' BETT-
YOU HEAR THAT?!

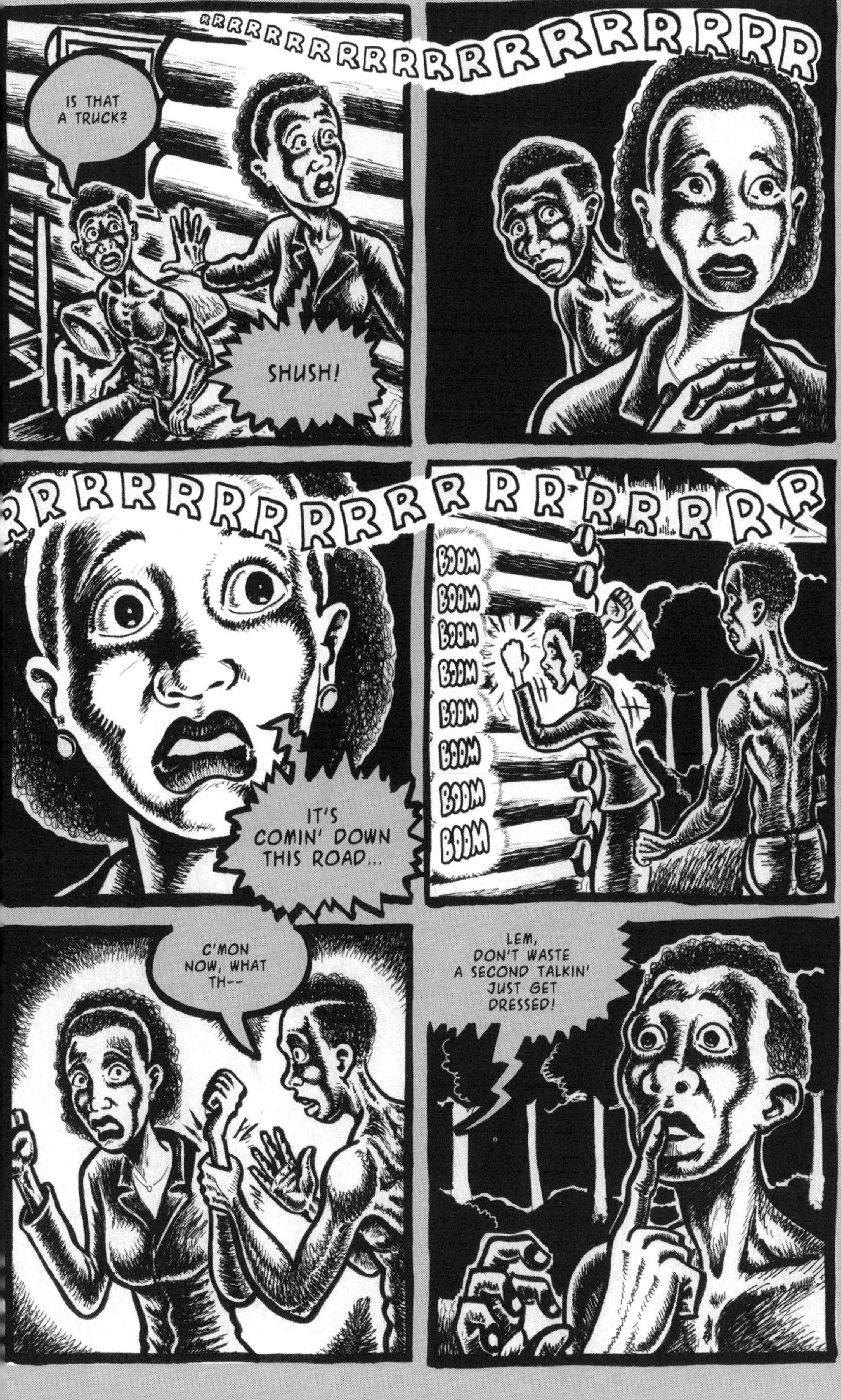
RRRRRRRRRRRRRRRRRRRR
IS THAT A TRUCK?
SHUSH!
RRRRRRRRRRRRRRRRRRRRRR
IT'S COMIN' DOWN THIS ROAD...
BOOM
BOOM
BOOM
BOOM
BOOM
BOOM
BOOM
BOOM
C'MON NOW, WHAT TH--
LEM, DON'T WASTE A SECOND TALKIN' JUST GET DRESSED!

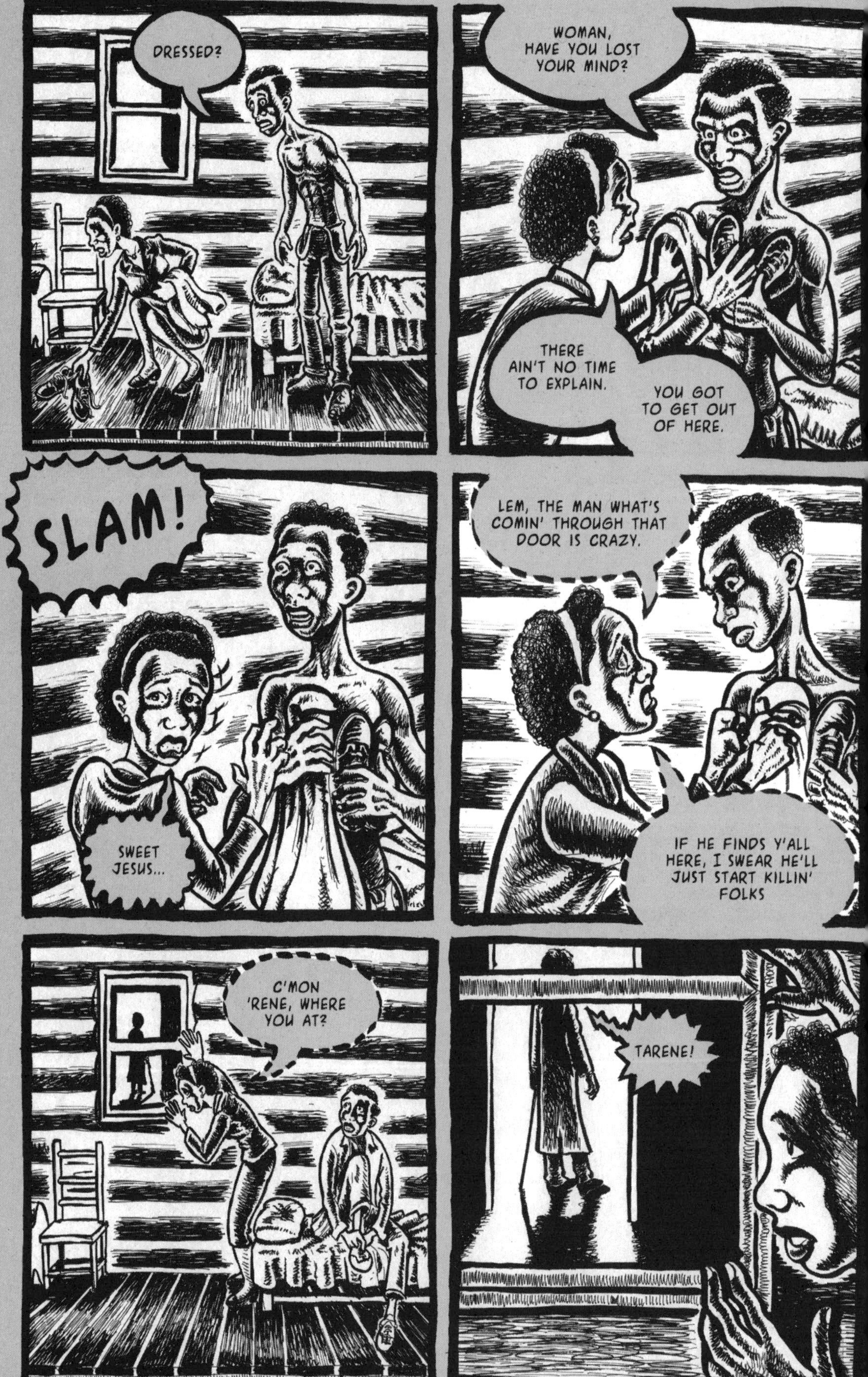
DRESSED?
WOMAN, HAVE YOU LOST YOUR MIND?
THERE AIN'T NO TIME TO EXPLAIN.
YOU GOT TO GET OUT OF HERE.
SLAM!
SWEET JESUS...
LEM, THE MAN WHAT'S COMIN' THROUGH THAT DOOR IS CRAZY.
IF HE FINDS Y'ALL HERE, I SWEAR HE'LL JUST START KILLIN' FOLKS
C'MON 'RENE, WHERE YOU AT?
TARENE!

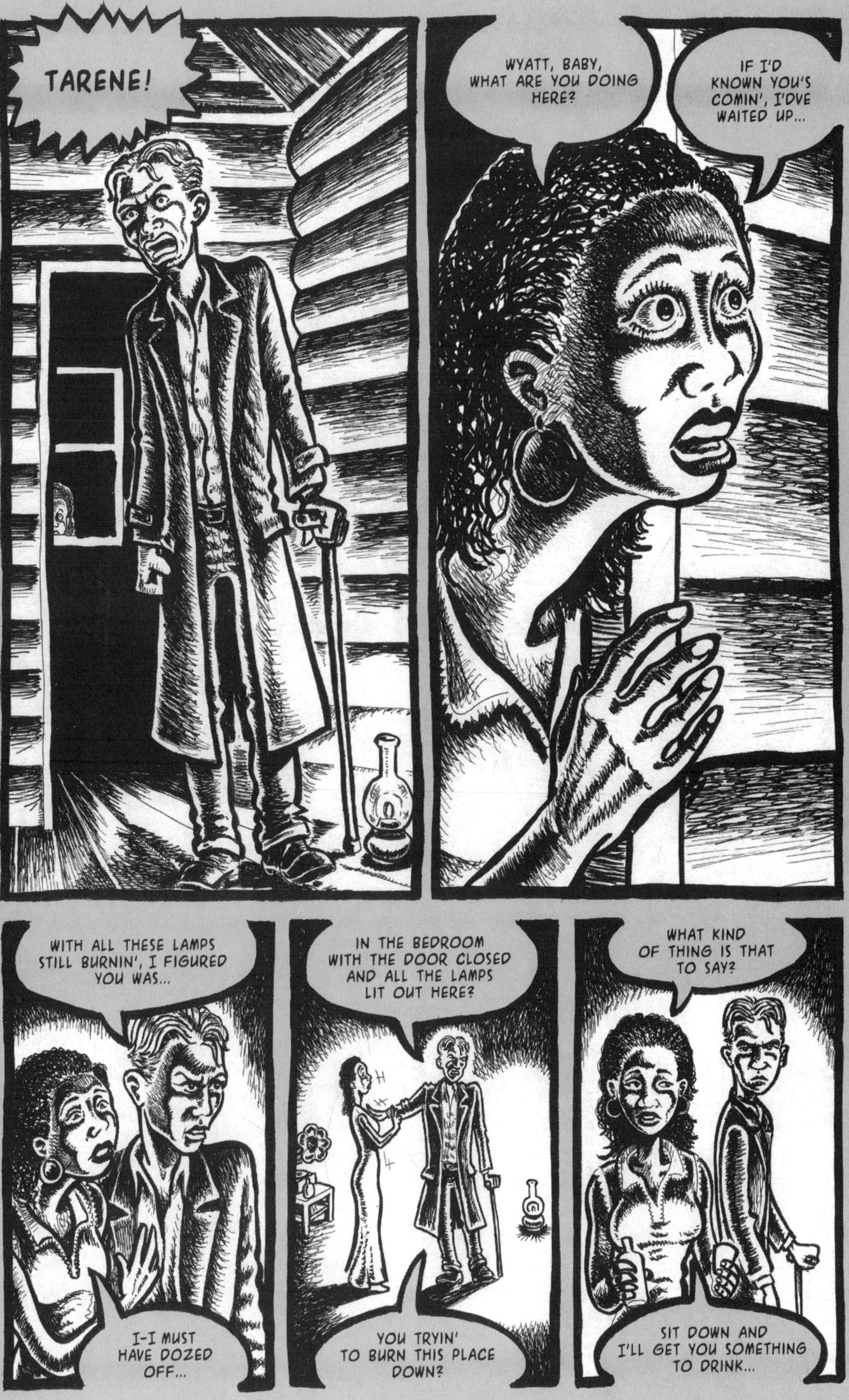
TARENE!
WYATT, BABY, WHAT ARE YOU DOING HERE?
IF I'D KNOWN YOU'S COMIN', I'DVE WAITED UP...
WITH ALL THESE LAMPS STILL BURNIN', I FIGURED YOU WAS...
I-I MUST HAVE DOZED OFF...
IN THE BEDROOM WITH THE DOOR CLOSED AND ALL THE LAMPS LIT OUT HERE?
YOU TRYIN' TO BURN THIS PLACE DOWN?
WHAT KIND OF THING IS THAT TO SAY?
SIT DOWN AND I'LL GET YOU SOMETHING TO DRINK...

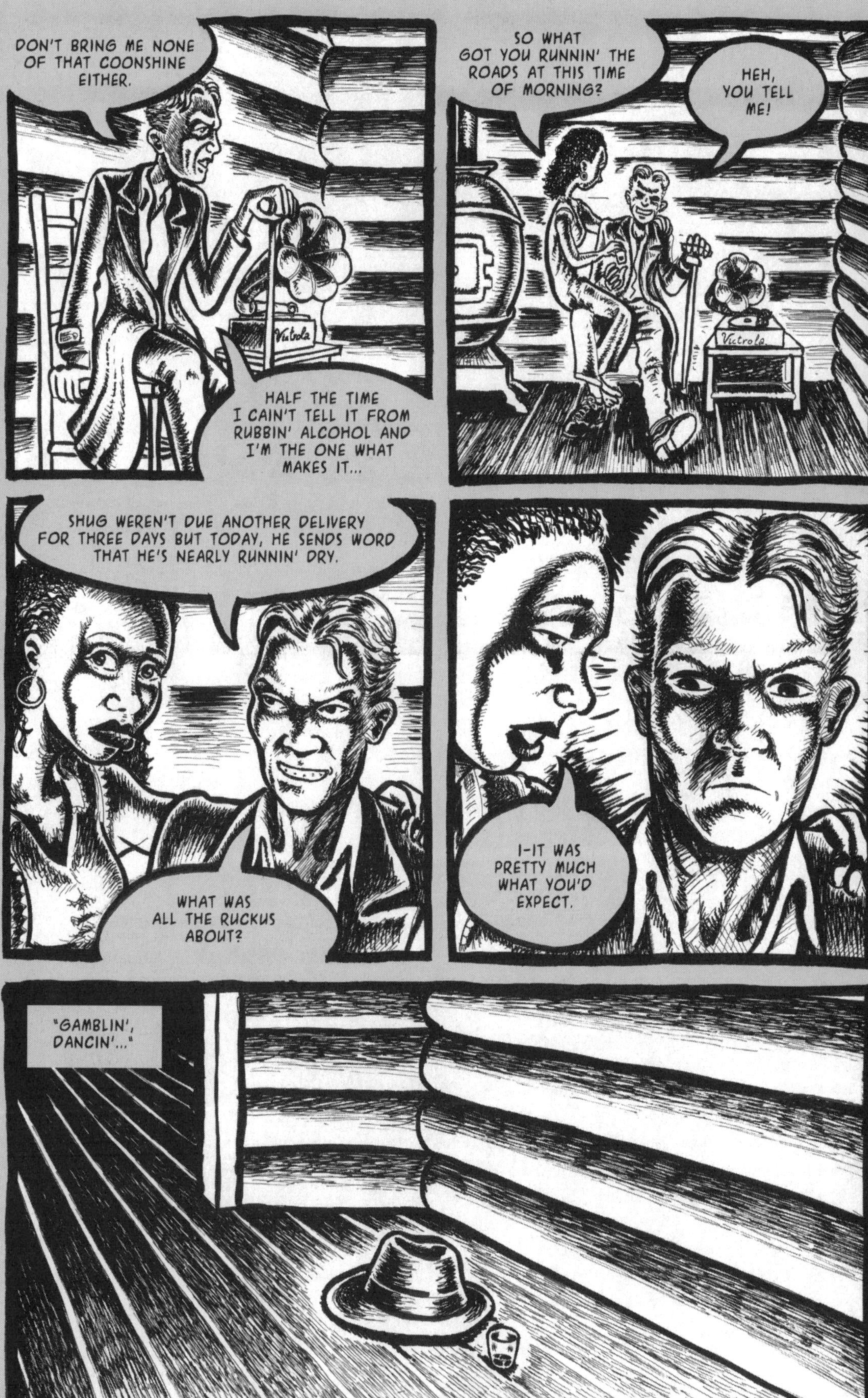
DON'T BRING ME NONE OF THAT COONSHINE EITHER.
HALF THE TIME I CAIN'T TELL IT FROM RUBBIN' ALCOHOL AND I'M THE ONE WHAT MAKES IT...
Victrola
SO WHAT GOT YOU RUNNIN' THE ROADS AT THIS TIME OF MORNING?
HEH, YOU TELL ME!
Victrola
SHUG WEREN'T DUE ANOTHER DELIVERY FOR THREE DAYS BUT TODAY, HE SENDS WORD THAT HE'S NEARLY RUNNIN' DRY.
WHAT WAS ALL THE RUCKUS ABOUT?
I-IT WAS PRETTY MUCH WHAT YOU'D EXPECT.
"GAMBLIN', DANCIN'..."

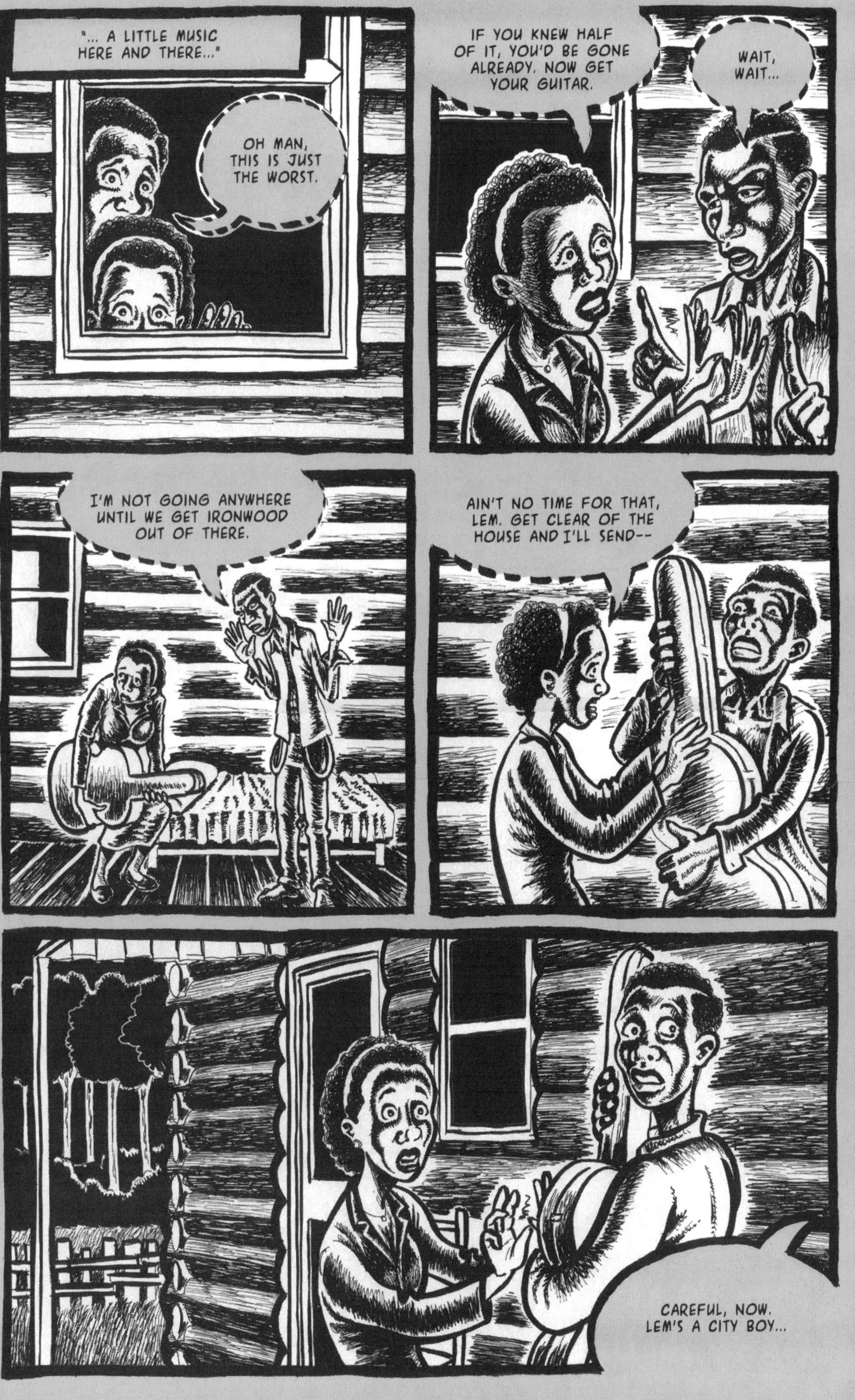
"... A LITTLE MUSIC HERE AND THERE..."
OH MAN, THIS IS JUST THE WORST.
IF YOU KNEW HALF OF IT, YOU'D BE GONE ALREADY. NOW GET YOUR GUITAR.
WAIT, WAIT...
I'M NOT GOING ANYWHERE UNTIL WE GET IRONWOOD OUT OF THERE.
AIN'T NO TIME FOR THAT, LEM. GET CLEAR OF THE HOUSE AND I'LL SEND--
CAREFUL, NOW. LEM'S A CITY BOY...

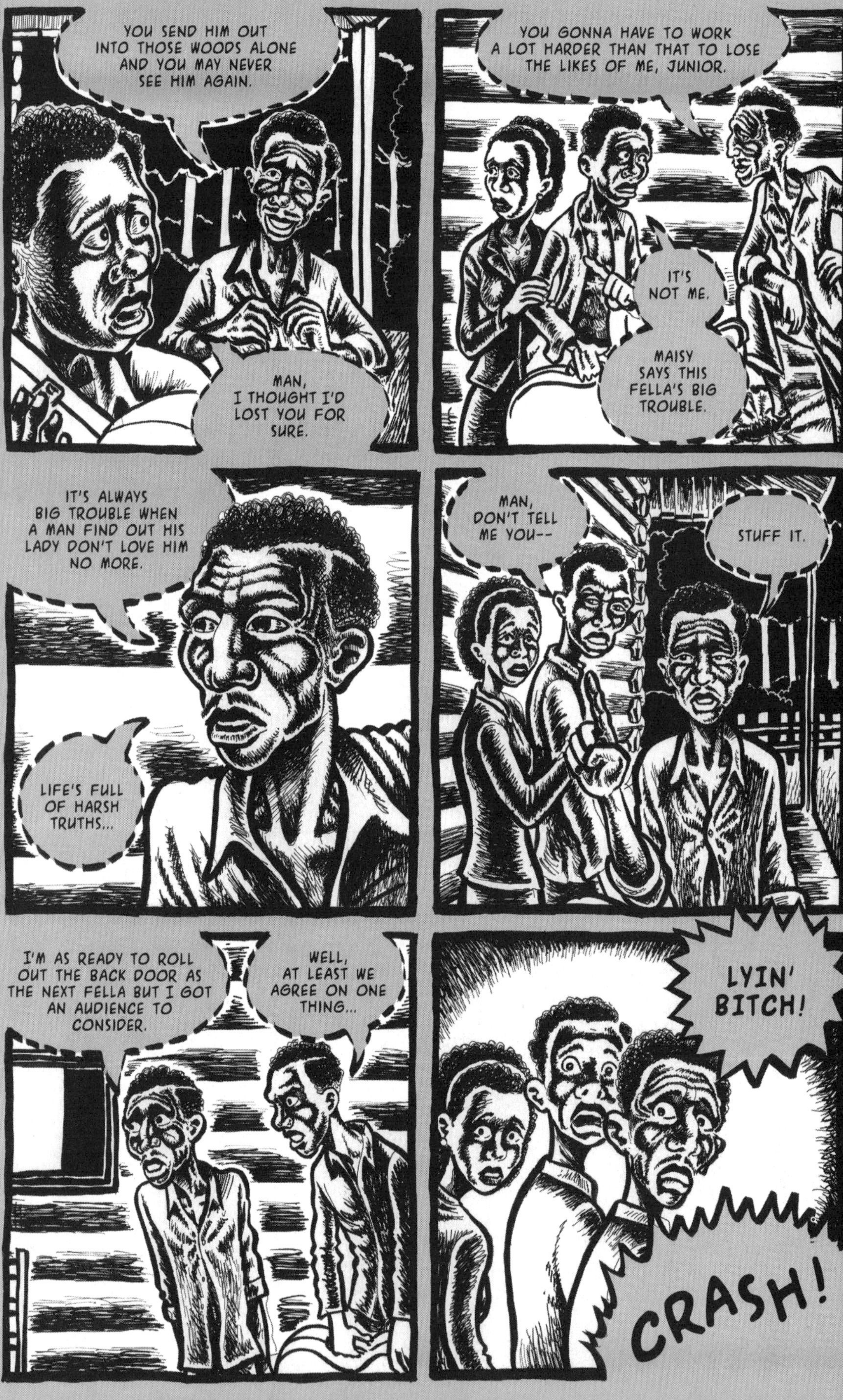
YOU SEND HIM OUT INTO THOSE WOODS ALONE AND YOU MAY NEVER SEE HIM AGAIN.
MAN, I THOUGHT I'D LOST YOU FOR SURE.
YOU GONNA HAVE TO WORK A LOT HARDER THAN THAT TO LOSE THE LIKES OF ME, JUNIOR.
IT'S NOT ME.
MAISY SAYS THIS FELLA'S BIG TROUBLE.
IT'S ALWAYS BIG TROUBLE WHEN A MAN FIND OUT HIS LADY DON'T LOVE HIM NO MORE.
LIFE'S FULL OF HARSH TRUTHS...
MAN, DON'T TELL ME YOU--
STUFF IT.
I'M AS READY TO ROLL OUT THE BACK DOOR AS THE NEXT FELLA BUT I GOT AN AUDIENCE TO CONSIDER.
WELL, AT LEAST WE AGREE ON ONE THING...
LYIN' BITCH!
CRASH!

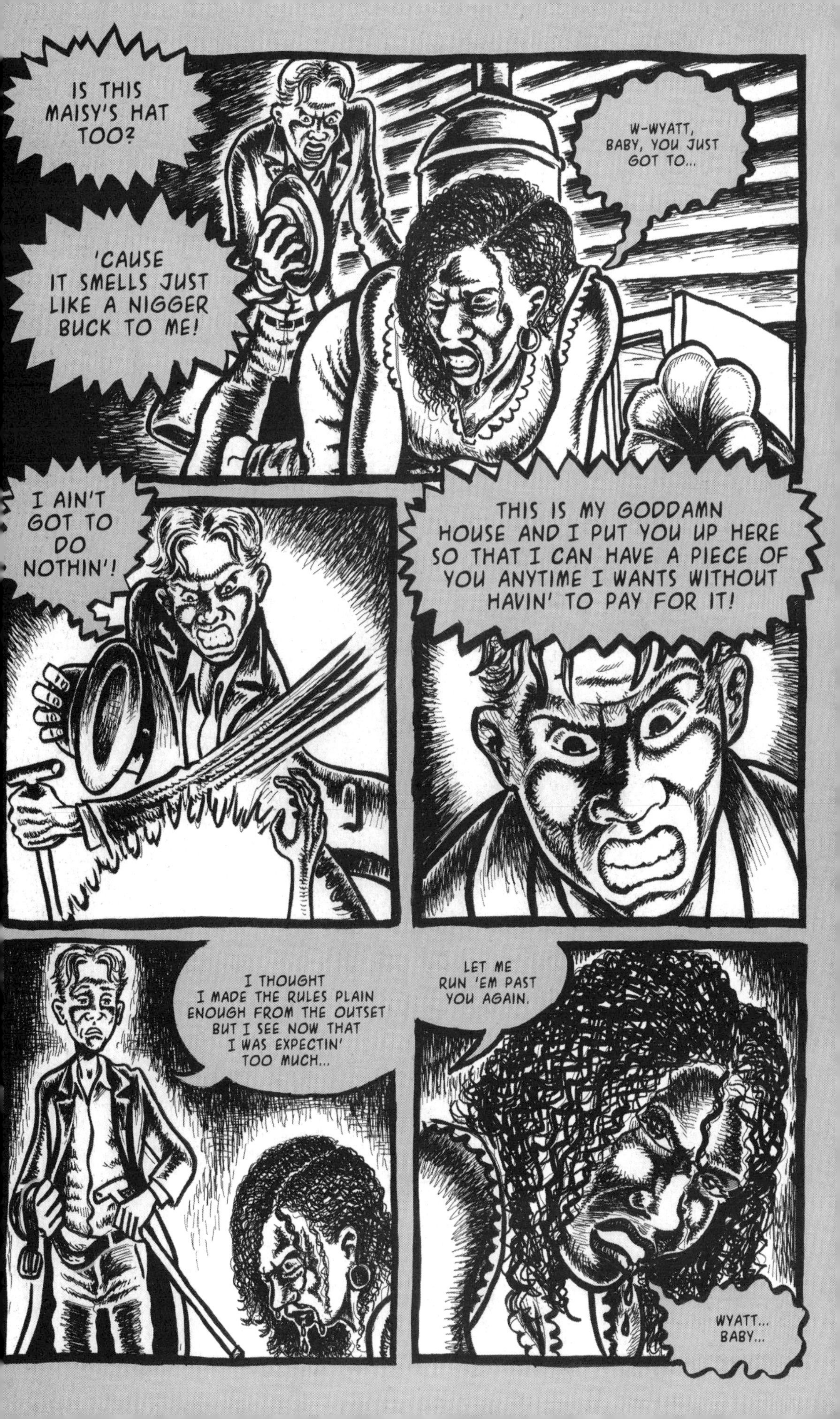
IS THIS MAISY'S HAT TOO?
W-WYATT, BABY, YOU JUST GOT TO...
'CAUSE IT SMELLS JUST LIKE A NIGGER BUCK TO ME!
I AIN'T GOT TO DO NOTHIN'!
THIS IS MY GODDAMN HOUSE AND I PUT YOU UP HERE SO THAT I CAN HAVE A PIECE OF YOU ANYTIME I WANTS WITHOUT HAVIN' TO PAY FOR IT!
I THOUGHT I MADE THE RULES PLAIN ENOUGH FROM THE OUTSET BUT I SEE NOW THAT I WAS EXPECTIN' TOO MUCH...
LET ME RUN 'EM PAST YOU AGAIN.
WYATT... BABY...

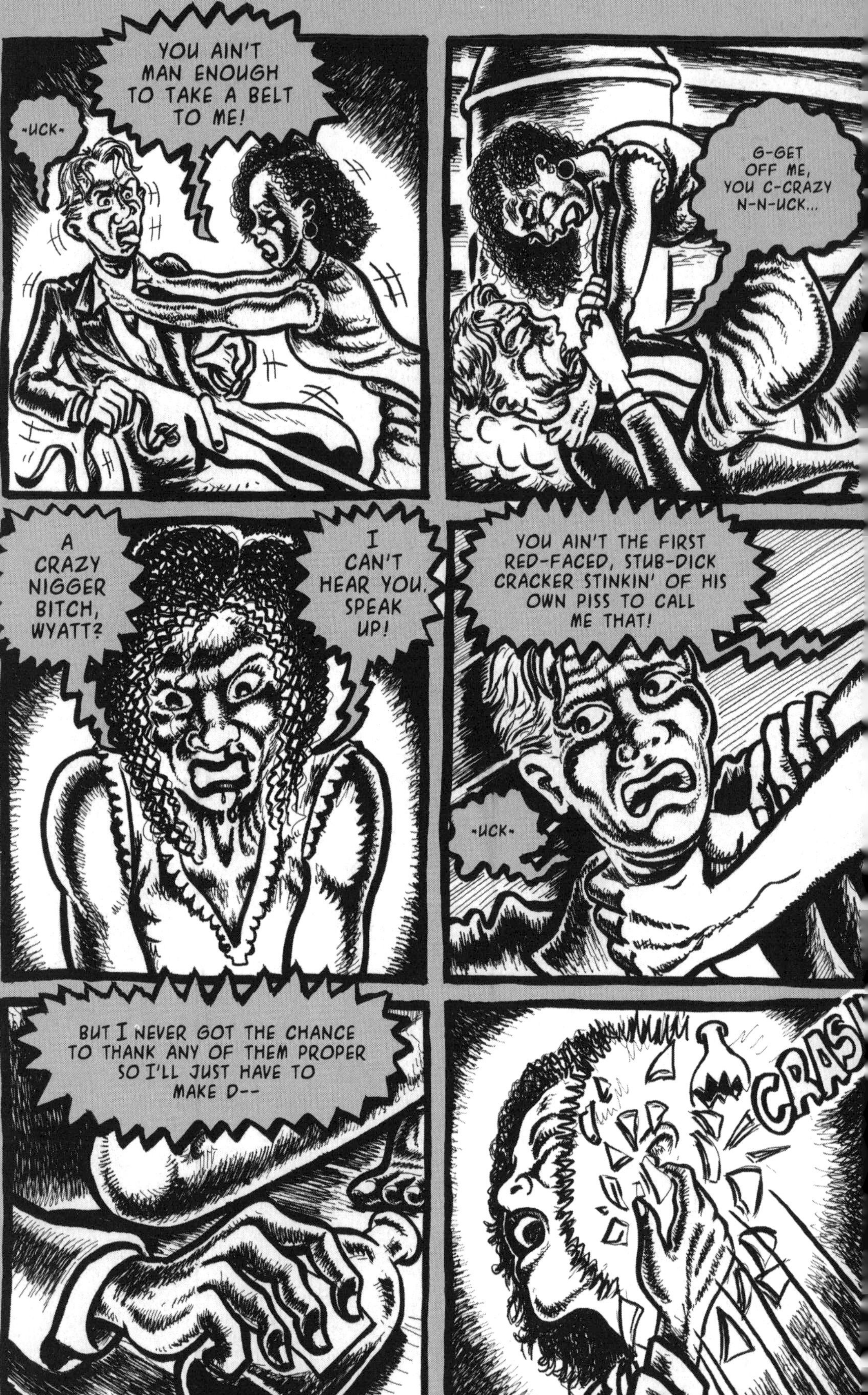

YOU AIN'T MAN ENOUGH TO TAKE A BELT TO ME!
-UCK-
G-GET OFF ME, YOU C-CRAZY N-N-UCK...
A CRAZY NIGGER BITCH, WYATT?
I CAN'T HEAR YOU. SPEAK UP!
YOU AIN'T THE FIRST RED-FACED, STUB-DICK CRACKER STINKIN' OF HIS OWN PISS TO CALL ME THAT!
-UCK-
BUT I NEVER GOT THE CHANCE TO THANK ANY OF THEM PROPER SO I'LL JUST HAVE TO MAKE D--
CRAS

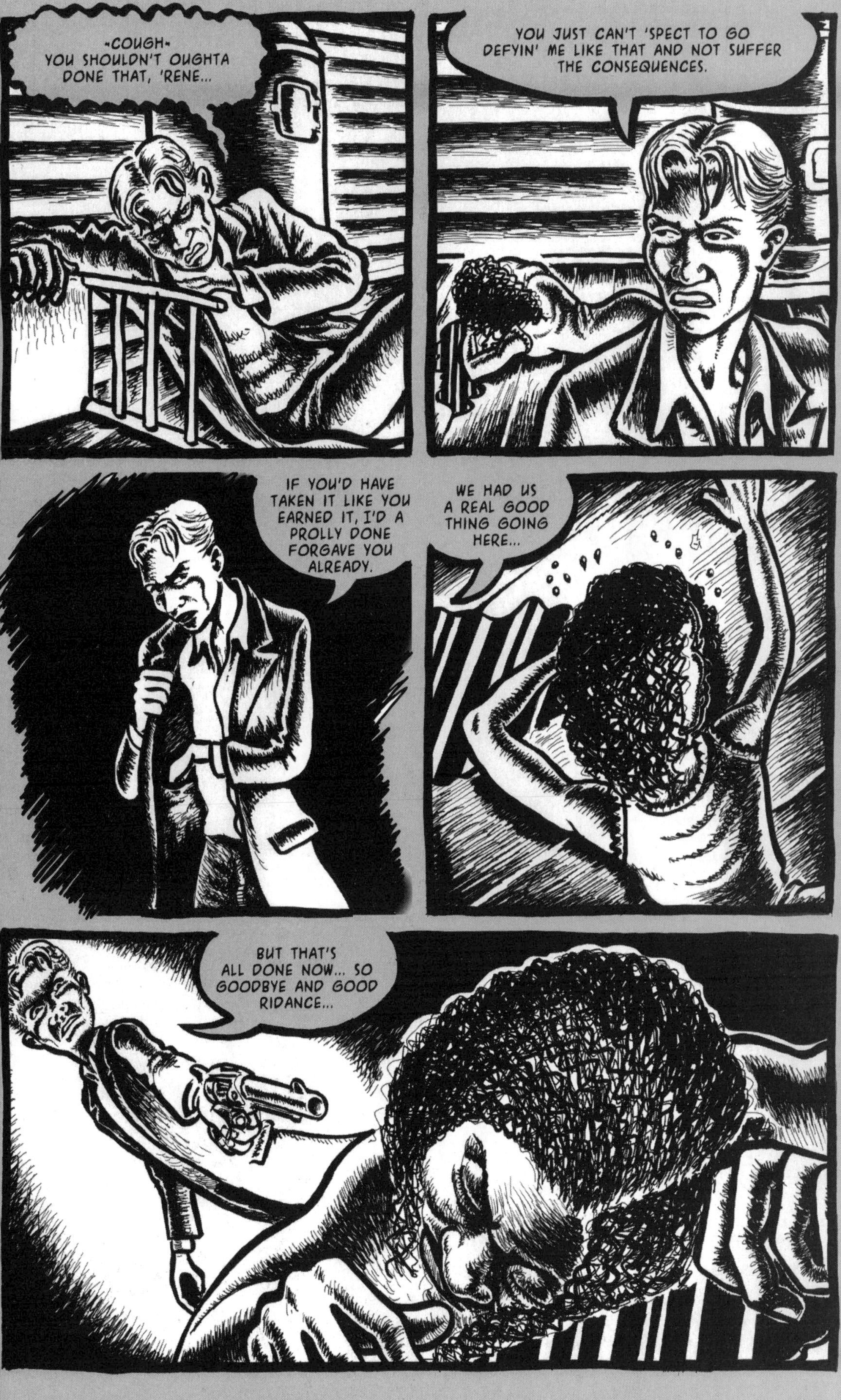

•COUGH•
YOU SHOULDN'T OUGHTA DONE THAT, 'RENE...
YOU JUST CAN'T 'SPECT TO GO DEFYIN' ME LIKE THAT AND NOT SUFFER THE CONSEQUENCES.
IF YOU'D HAVE TAKEN IT LIKE YOU EARNED IT, I'D A PROLLY DONE FORGAVE YOU ALREADY.
WE HAD US A REAL GOOD THING GOING HERE...
BUT THAT'S ALL DONE NOW... SO GOODBYE AND GOOD RIDANCE...

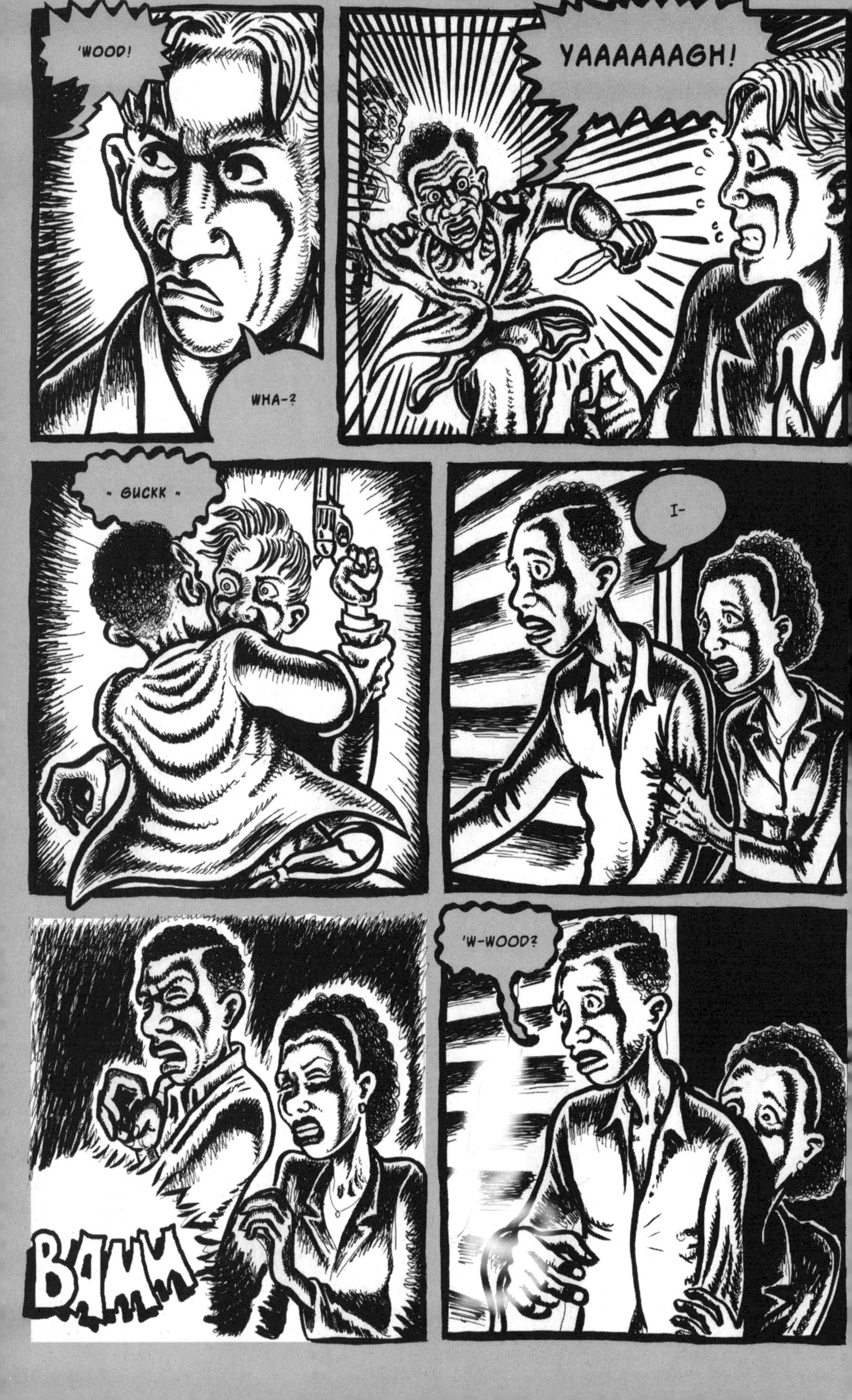
'WOOD!
WHA-?
YAAAAAAGH!
~ GUCKK ~
I-
BAMM
'W-WOOD?

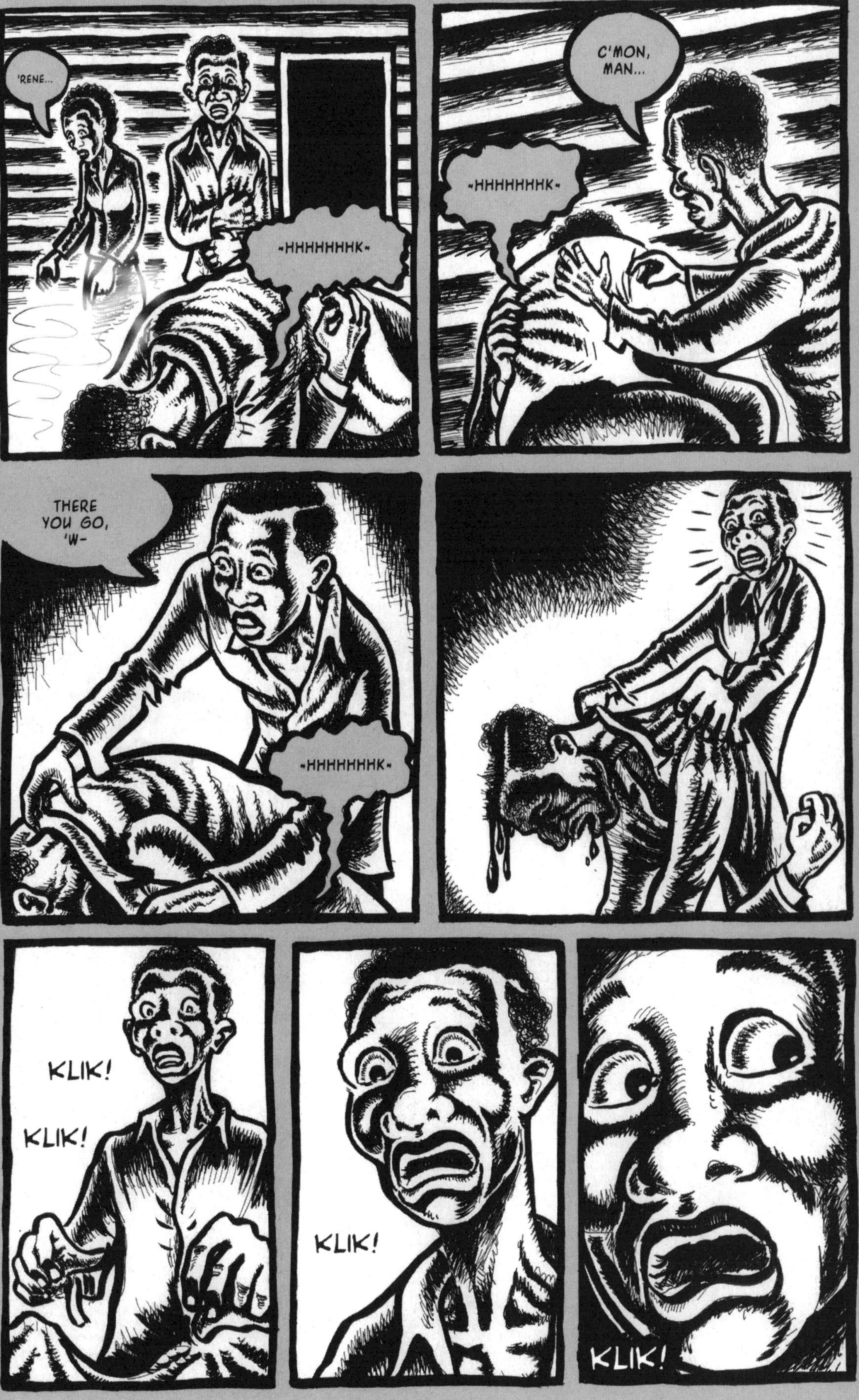
'RENE...
«HHHHHHHK»
C'MON, MAN...
«HHHHHHHK»
THERE YOU GO, 'W-
«HHHHHHHK»
KLIK!
KLIK!
KLIK!
KLIK!

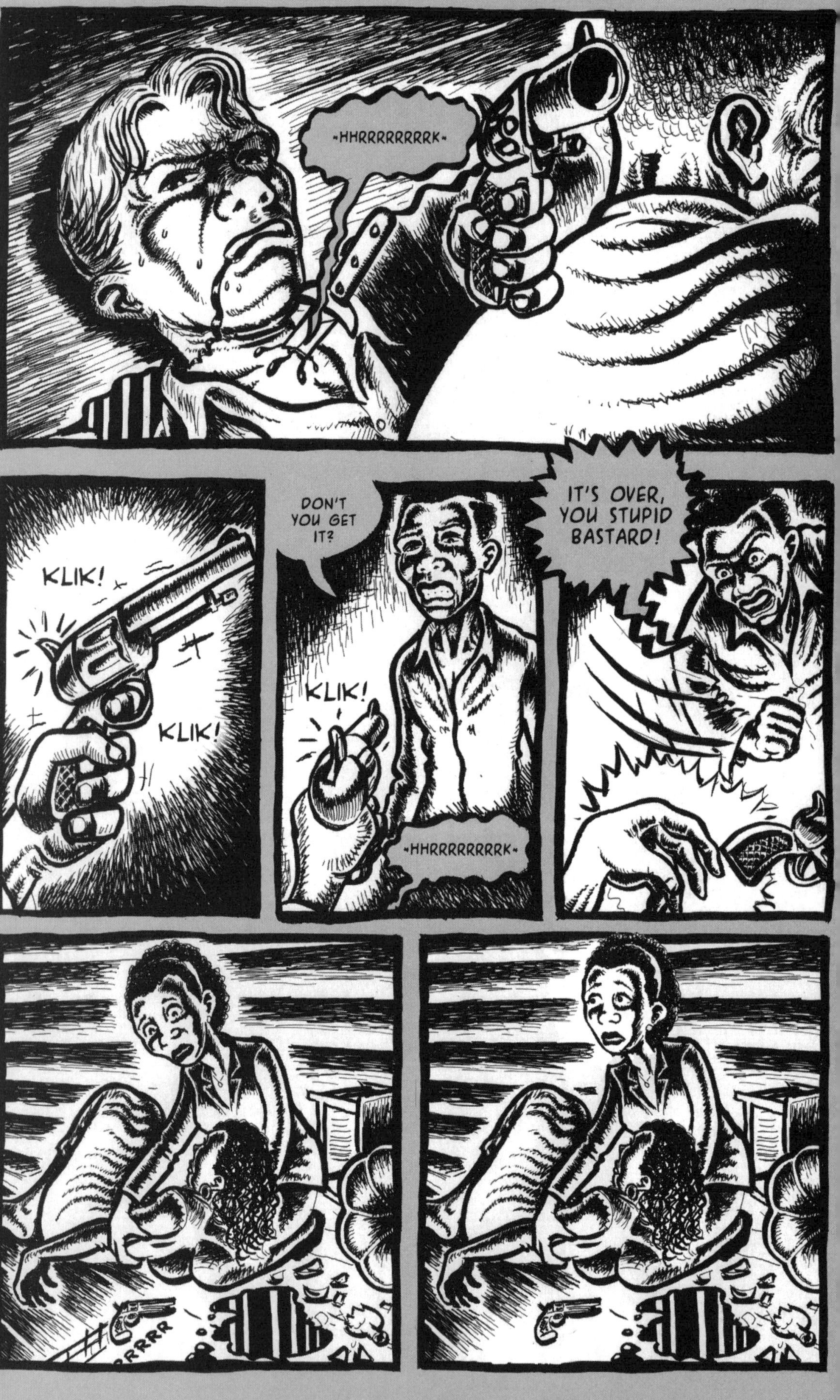

"HHRRRRRRRRK"
KLIK!
KLIK!
DON'T YOU GET IT?
KLIK!
"HHRRRRRRRRK"
IT'S OVER, YOU STUPID BASTARD!
RRRR

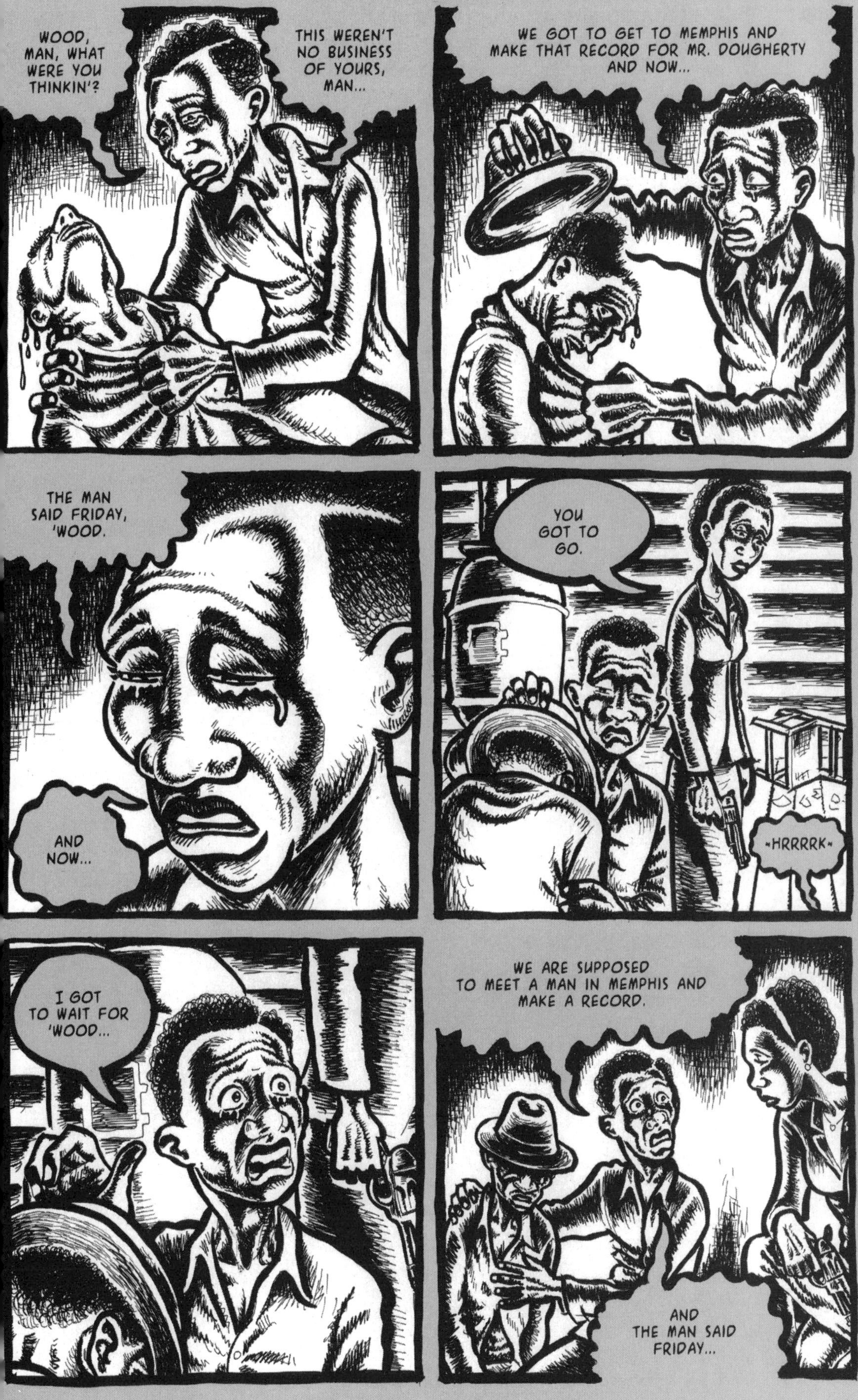
WOOD, MAN, WHAT WERE YOU THINKIN'?
THIS WEREN'T NO BUSINESS OF YOURS, MAN...
WE GOT TO GET TO MEMPHIS AND MAKE THAT RECORD FOR MR. DOUGHERTY AND NOW...
THE MAN SAID FRIDAY, 'WOOD.
AND NOW...
YOU GOT TO GO.
»HRRRRK«
I GOT TO WAIT FOR 'WOOD...
WE ARE SUPPOSED TO MEET A MAN IN MEMPHIS AND MAKE A RECORD.
AND THE MAN SAID FRIDAY...

I-I THINK THERE'S BEEN A MURDER...

I KNOW. YOU GOT TO GO, LEM...

... 'CAUSE THERE'S FITTIN' TO BE ANOTHER".

"AND TOMORROW AFTER THE WHITE FOLKS COME AND SEE WHAT BEEN DONE..."

"WON'T BE NO END TO ALL THE KILLIN'..."

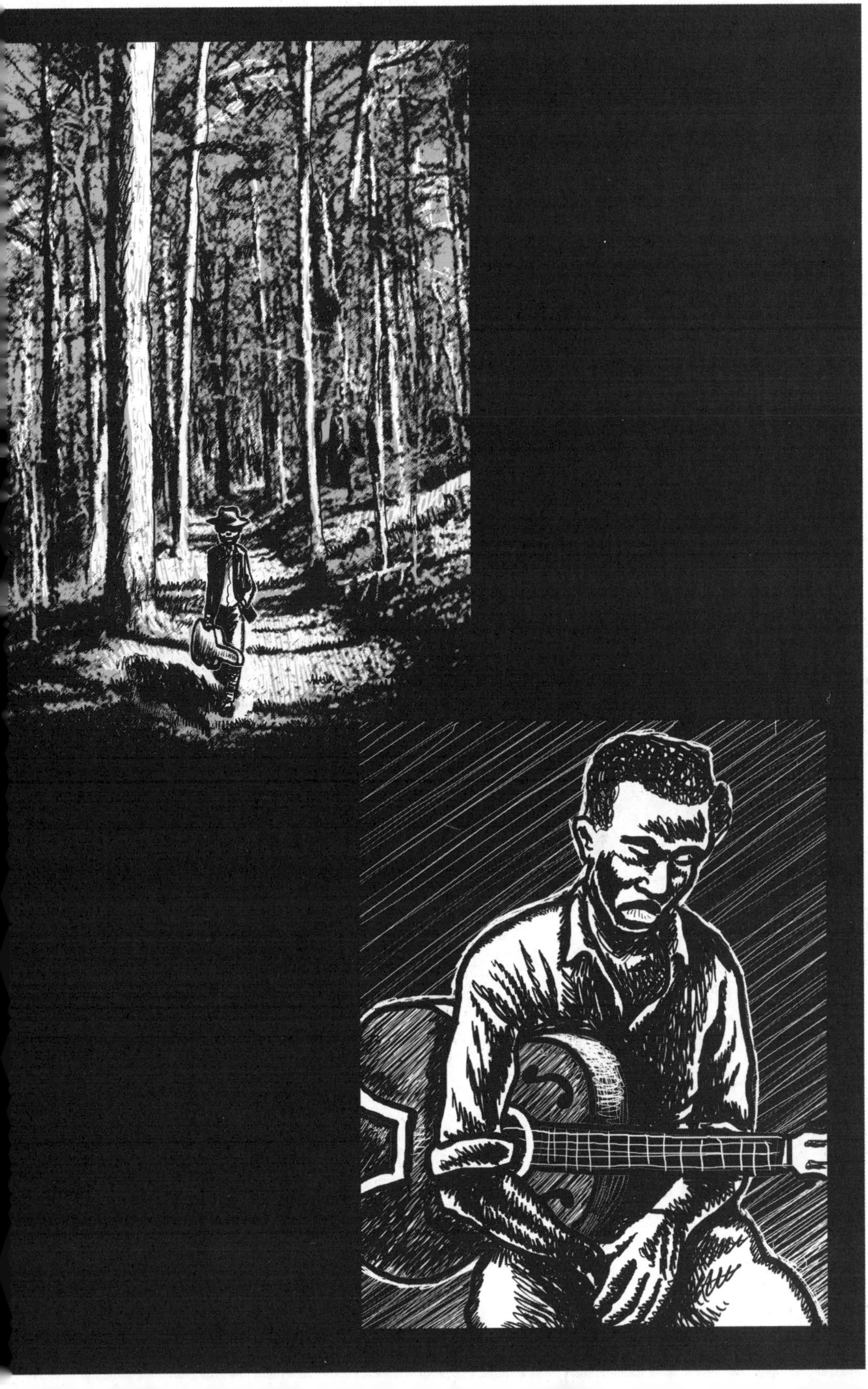

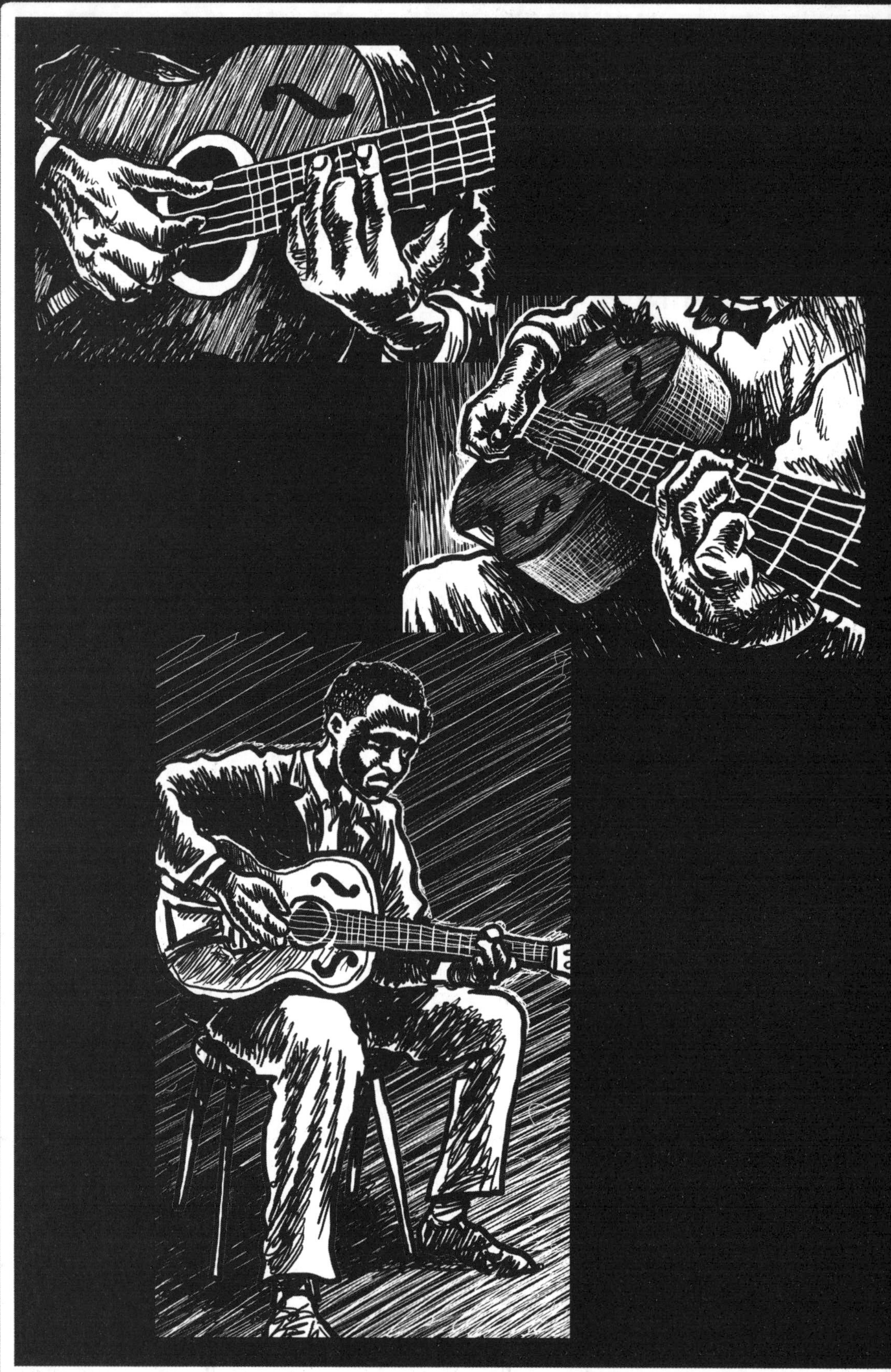